Falling For Her Cowboy

Silver Creek Ranch
Book 9

Peyton Banks

The Silver Creek Ranch

Forgotten military heroes who needed a helping hand re-entering the society they had been sworn to protect. The Silver Creek Ranch provided a space where these cowboys could work the land and get back in touch with the men they once were.

The battles of war left scars on each of them.

Healing was what these cowboys needed.

Who knew it would comprise the touch, kiss, and love of a good woman?

The Silver Creek Ranch is an interracial cowboy romance shared world. Each captivating story is filled with plenty of heat and will leave your heart racing with the desire to devour every one of them.

Falling For Her Cowboy
Blurb

***She came to Silver Creek Ranch for peace.
She never expected to find love in the arms
of the local vet.***

After losing everything in the military—her fiancé, her identity, and her hard-won reputation—Melah Battle was desperate for a fresh start. Silver Creek Ranch offered a quiet escape and a place to rebuild. But peace was hard to hold onto when the past refused to let go.

Ridge Harvey, the local veterinarian, wasn't looking for love. But one late-night emergency and a pair of soulful brown eyes changed everything. From the moment he met Melah, Ridge was drawn to her strength and the undeniable spark between them.

Silver Creek had seen its share of people running from pain, and Ridge knew better than most what it meant to carry scars. But something about Melah made him want to break down her walls and offer her more than just comfort.

He was determined to give her protection, happiness... and a love worth staying for.

Falling for Her Cowboy is a steamy interracial BWWM romance with a resilient heroine, a protective small town hero and a HEA!

Chapter One

"Stop! Please. Stop," Melah cried out. She squeezed her eyes shut and tried to ignore the pain. Her breaths came fast while fear engulfed her. Darkness consumed her as she fought to get away from him. Another strangled cry burst from her.

Not again.

She attempted to move her arms, but they were restricted. She struggled even harder to break free from whatever held her down. She turned to run away but slammed into something rigid and unforgiving. The air in her lungs flew out of her from the impact.

"Melah!" a familiar voice called her name.

Melah froze and inhaled sharply. Something was

different. She moved her arms again, and this time they were free. She reached out and felt around. There was something hard underneath her. She opened her eyes and blinked.

She was on the floor.

Not the dirty ground of the desert. Melah Battle lifted her head and took in the blurred vision of a woman standing in the doorway patiently waiting for her to get her bearings. She blinked again to get her gaze to focus.

It was Aimee, one of the hands at the Silver Creek Ranch.

Melah exhaled and dropped her head to the floor in embarrassment. She didn't even want to know what was going through Aimee's mind.

"You okay, there?" Aimee asked. She hadn't come fully into the room. She waited by the door for Melah's answer.

"Yeah. Just another nightmare," Melah answered quietly. She squeezed her eyes shut and inhaled. Why did this keep happening? Why couldn't she shake the nightmares? It had been a few years since that night.

"Need any help getting off the floor? I heard you cry out. I figured I'd better come and make sure you were alone in here," Aimee said.

Melah glanced up again. Aimee held a small gun. Melah felt damn good that her fellow female cowhand was coming to protect her if need be.

"I got it." She pushed up off the floor and winced. She glanced over at the bed where her blankets were all askew. The scarf that had been wrapped around her head was on the floor. She bent down and snatched it up. "I hope I didn't wake you."

"I was up. I have a hard time sleeping. You know. Nightmares." Aimee shrugged.

She leaned against the doorframe and stared at Melah. She was slightly older than Melah and had been very welcoming when Melah had arrived at the ranch. She'd been there two months longer than her. With them being the only women working the ranch, they had already started to get to know one another in the two weeks that Melah had been there.

"Thanks for coming to check on me. What time is it?" Melah glanced around at the small room that held a couple of bunks. It was one of two sleeping rooms. This was the women's bunkhouse where they could stay on the Silver Creek Ranch. They'd each taken a room.

"It's a little after four." Aimee yawned.

"I think I'm going to go for a run. I'm not going to be able to go back to sleep," Melah said. Nor did she want to. This dream had been all too real, and it had shaken her to the core.

She walked over to her nightstand and turned on the lamp. She snagged her smart watch off its charger, strapped it on, and moved over to one of the dressers. She didn't have many clothes here. It had been pointless to bring tons of stuff. She hadn't planned to be on the ranch long, nor did she think she'd be settling down in Ironhaven.

What had she planned for when she left here? She had no idea. It was just her and her horse she had to worry about.

But for now, she was going to take advantage of everything the ranch had to offer women like her and take each day in stride. She had plenty of time to figure out her next move. She'd saved up some money when she'd been in the service.

"You be careful out there. I'm going to try to get some shut-eye before my shift." Aimee pushed off the doorframe and waved.

"Goodnight."

Aimee shut the door, leaving Melah alone. She opened the drawer and eyed her measly clothing. She had plenty of Army t-shirts and grimaced. Maybe she should invest in new clothing. Something that didn't advertise how she had spent most of her life.

She fingered the soft gray shirt and sighed.

Twenty years of her life had been dedicated to the military. At eighteen she had decided she'd follow in her father's footsteps and enter the service. She smiled, remembering the day as if it were yesterday. Vernon Battle had been a proud dad down at the recruiter's office. His smile had been wide and bright as she'd echoed the oath to serve.

It had been a tough decision. Life as an Army brat hadn't been glamorous. Hell, life for the two of them had been tough. It had been just her and Vernon while she grew up. Vernon was lucky to have the support of his brother and sister-in-law. Melah and Vernon had moved around a lot. She'd gotten the opportunity to live all around the world, and when he was deployed, she'd go and stay with her uncle and aunt. Even though they hadn't had much, Melah appreciated what she did have.

She snagged the shirt from the drawer and opened another one for a pair of shorts. She hurried and got dressed, dipping into the bathroom to make herself decent. After her run she'd shower before she reported to work.

"He can't hurt me anymore." She wouldn't

mention *he who shall not be named.* Her life had been a living hell, but she had taken it back.

She brushed her thick hair up into a high ponytail. She set the brush on the counter and stared at her reflection. Her big brown eyes were wide. Her tawny skin was flawless, thanks to her skin routine. No longer was she the skinny young girl with acne and blackheads when she'd first enlisted.

She was now more mature with a curvy frame toned from her workouts. She may not be in the Army any longer, but that didn't mean she gave up on keeping in shape. She cleaned up her mess she had created and stored her belongings in the drawer. She exited the bathroom, snagged her fanny pack and cellphone, then made her way through the house. She left the building and breathed in the fresh South Dakota air.

The sky was painted a multitude of orange hues as the sun prepared to rise. Now she was able to inhale the fresh air, her nerves calmed slightly. She clipped her pack onto her waist then unzipped it to obtain her earbuds. She'd need to listen to some music to help keep her mind from wandering back to her dream. Once she found a good playlist, she tossed her phone in the pack and zipped it up. After doing a few light stretches, she began her trek.

The Silver Creek Ranch was a grand spread. She was lucky to find such a place to stay after she'd retired from the Army. The ranch had come highly recommended, and she was thankful that it was shared with her. This was what she needed to start the second phase of her life.

Melah loved to run. It allowed her to have time to herself and work out the kinks in her body. It always gave her a sense of freedom with the wind gently blowing in her face and the marvelous sprawling lands that surrounded her. She loved the feeling of her muscles relaxing and her feet pounding on the ground. The dirt road wasn't ideal, but it would do. It honestly reminded her of the runs she and a few of her battalion members had gone on when deployed or stationed somewhere away from civilization.

She missed her friends like crazy. Terri, Issac, and Cora had been her closest, and they had stood by her side through the toughest time in her life. She inhaled sharply and pushed down those memories. Instead, her last night as a member of the US Army came to mind. Her friends had surprised her with a retirement party of just the four of them. They were the siblings she'd never had.

That night, they'd gone out to a local bar where

they'd consumed plenty of alcohol and good food. She smiled at the memory and made a mental note to reach out to them. They were still enlisted. Terri wanted to do another year or two before submitting her paperwork, while Issac and Cora were both staying in until they reached retirement eligibility. Melah had been in the longest. She missed them fiercely. She could see Issac out here on the ranch riding a horse. He'd love it. He was a Texan at heart, and they both had a love for horses. Terri and Cora were city girls, from Atlanta and Chicago. Neither would be caught dead mucking stalls or roping cattle.

She grinned. How the two of them survived the Army, she didn't know, but there was no one else she'd trust to have her six than Terri, Cora, and Issac.

Melah pushed herself faster. She ignored the burn in her lungs. She was going to have a great day today. She wasn't going to allow a little nightmare to get to her.

She was stronger than that. She'd proven it with everything life had thrown her way. Melah Battle would figure out life. She took in the acres of land and the cattle off in the distance.

Right now, this was where she belonged and she felt safe here. The men and women she'd met and worked with respected her and made her feel welcome.

This was her new beginning.

* * *

"Do you want to comment?"

All eyes turned to Melah. She swallowed hard and looked around the circle of ten men sitting in the room. It was late afternoon after work, and she'd decided to attend a group therapy session offered on the ranch. These men were like her. Former military and needing help getting back on their feet.

"Umm..." Her mind drew a blank at what to say. Her heart fluttered as her anxiety flared to life.

"It's okay. You don't have to say much. How about a short introduction." Spencer was the social worker who led the therapy sessions each week. He pushed his round glasses higher onto the bridge of his nose.

This was the third session Melah had attended, but she hadn't really participated. She'd just observed, not yet comfortable to contribute. There were tons of hands working the ranch. Today she recognized some of the guys.

If she was going to stride toward a new life, she

had to get out of her comfort zone. It wouldn't be fair for others to pour out their feelings while she remained quiet and not sharing. She needed this. Therapy was supposed to help her. She sat up straighter and jerked her head in a nod.

Spencer smiled and motioned for her to start. She glanced around the group and didn't see anyone judging her for being there. Her gaze landed on Trent. He had helped show her the ropes when she'd first arrived. From the short time she'd worked with him she'd learned he was an Army man—a Ranger.

"Hi. I'm Melah," she said.

"Hello, Melah," the guys all echoed together.

A few nodded in her direction. She paused, unsure where to start. She thought back to how some of them had just done a basic introduction and figured she'd follow suit.

"I'm from Dunwich, Missouri. A small town west of Jefferson City. I recently retired from the Army." She exhaled and chuckled at the claps she received. She missed the town she was from. Her family was still there. She thought of the welcome home party they'd thrown her when she'd returned home. They sure made a girl feel special. It had been just what she'd needed. To be surrounded by friends and family.

"Retired? You don't look a day over twenty-five." Trent folded his arms and tossed her a wink.

She rolled her eyes playfully. This wasn't the first time she'd heard that remark. She was proud of her twenty years she'd served. No one would be able to take that away from her.

"I may not look it, but my body reminds me every day." She sat up straighter and made sure she met everyone's gaze. "I know I haven't said much. I do thank you all for sharing your stories. I'm going to try my best to participate more."

"That's wonderful, Melah. There is no judgment here amongst us. This is a safe space to share whatever may be troubling you. If you need to come get something off your chest, we are here to listen," Spencer said.

Nods went around again. That made her feel better. In the sessions she had attended, she'd heard stories that tugged at her heartstrings. One thing they all had in common was trying to pick up the pieces of what was left after serving in the military.

"Thanks. I really appreciate that."

"Hell, and if it's during the middle of the day and shit's getting you down, you find one of us. We're all here in this together," another cowboy with his wide-brimmed hat resting on his knee spoke up.

She hadn't caught his name and didn't recognize him. He had salt-and-pepper hair with a thick mustache.

"My name is Henry, but all my friends call me Cash."

"You can grab me, too," Trent offered.

She murmured her thanks, and emotions swelled in her chest. She prayed she didn't get teary-eyed and bawl like a baby. That was the last thing she needed. She wasn't one to cry much, but lately she'd been all up in her feelings. She'd caught herself on the verge of tears watching videos on social media. She was a tough chick. She'd been deployed several times. Trained in hand-to-hand combat. Had been on the front lines—she didn't cry.

"Thanks, guys," she said.

"One thing about Silver Creek, you are never alone."

Chapter Two

Ridge Harvey killed the engine to his pickup truck and got out. It was early in the morning, and already his stomach was notifying him he needed to fill it. The sun was barely on the horizon, but he was sure Ms. Bee had breakfast ready—or at least a steamy pot of hot coffee. He stalked to the front porch and froze in place at the sight that greeted him.

His older brother, Draven, stepped out of the house.

A grin stole across Ridge's face.

The two of them were close. Even though Draven was older by four years, it hadn't even mattered. He'd always included Ridge in everything he did. Ridge had been the wide-eyed kid trailing behind his big brother everywhere. Ridge had missed the hell out of him when he'd gone off and joined the Marines when they were younger. A part of him had been missing when Draven left for basic training. Their father, who had retired from the Army, had figured at least one of his boys would follow in his footsteps, but apparently the Marines had been for Draven while the Navy had been Ridge's calling.

"Mornin'," Ridge called out.

When Draven had first come home after retiring he'd had an edge to him. Years ago, they had all noticed a change in him. He had become harsher, colder, with a glint in his eyes that Ridge had seen in many of the soldiers he'd come to know. His sibling was dangerous. Ridge had heard whispers of Draven's deployments and missions. Whatever he had done in the service had certainly affected him.

Ridge had never asked. He just knew he had to work on getting his brother back.

"Mornin'," Draven murmured.

He had a large travel mug in his hand that Ridge was sure held Ms. Bee's famous coffee. Anything that woman touched in the kitchen was gold.

"Fancy seeing you here bright and early." Ridge walked up the stairs to the porch.

Draven leaned against the banister and stared

out into the yard. "Figured I'd get an early start today. I have a few things to do this afternoon with Cashea." He shrugged then sipped his coffee.

Ridge leaned against the pillar of the porch and held back a grin. Who would have thought Draven would be shacking up with a woman. With the way he'd been so antisocial and snarling at everyone, it was a miracle he'd caught Cashea's eye.

Ridge thought back to the day he'd first met Cashea. She'd been coming out of Draven's house early in the morning in an attempt to leave. It hadn't taken Ridge long to figure out why she was leaving so darn early. She'd had the guiltiest look when she'd discovered him outside.

She was a good woman and perfect for his grouch of a brother. The Marines may have changed Draven, but Cashea was definitely a positive in his life. He was coming around the family more, which was all Ridge wanted.

"Is the food ready?" Ridge patted himself on his flat stomach. The way it was rumbling, he could probably put away a few plates of food. If breakfast wasn't ready, he'd just stop somewhere on the way to his clinic. It wouldn't be as good as Ms. Bee's cooking, but he needed something to satisfy his hunger.

"You know Ms. Bee gets up earlier than any of us to make sure we're taken care of."

"Pops in there?" If their father was inside, then he could at least sit and eat with the old man.

Andy Harvey was a man Draven and Ridge looked up to. He was one of the strongest men Ridge knew. After their mother had died, Andy had to hold everything together for them. Not a day went by that Ridge didn't miss the sound of his mother's laughter. She'd be proud of them.

"Yeah. He just sat down at the table." Draven tipped his chin at Ridge. "I better go. I'm supposed to be meeting with some of the new hands so we can go out to the west pasture."

"I'll be around today after I do my calls," Ridge said. Even after working a full day in his veterinary clinic and making farm calls, he still chipped in around the ranch to help out. He slapped Draven on the shoulder and took notice that his brother didn't stiffen as he used to.

He was definitely making strides.

Draven jogged down the stairs and headed to his truck. Ridge grinned and stepped into the house. The scent of bacon greeted him and sent him moving faster toward the kitchen. The main house was where he and Draven had grown up. His mother,

God rest her soul, had made it a home. He had many fond memories of getting chased out of the house by her for tracking in dirt on her newly swept floors.

He missed that woman something fierce. It was a shame how something as ugly as cancer had barged into their lives and claimed the most graceful soul.

"Is that you, Ridge?" Bee's voice sailed through the air.

How the hell did that woman know he was in the house? He hadn't made too much noise. He arrived at the kitchen door and found Belinda "Bee" Butler standing at the stove stirring something in a large pot. She glanced over her shoulder and offered him a warm smile.

Bee had been a wonderful addition to the ranch. His father had hired her on a few years after his mother had passed. She was in charge of the cooking and cleaning at the main house and even cooked for the hands. Her homecooked meals were legendary and what many of the men and women who came through the ranch needed. There was a saying that food could soothe the soul, and Ms. Bee sure knew how to make a man feel whole with her cooking.

"Morning, Bee." His gaze landed on Andy and Buck sitting at the table. "Pops. Buck. Morning." He pushed off the doorframe and headed to the table.

The two older men echoed their greetings.

"Now don't you go sitting down at my table when you haven't washed your hands, young man," Bee announced.

Andy chuckled and tipped his coffee mug toward Ridge. "You know the rules."

Even Buck smiled slightly. His attention was on the newspaper in front of him. His plate barely showed any evidence that food had graced it.

"Yes, ma'am." Ridge spun on his heels and walked over to the sink. There would be no disrespecting Ms. Bee. He quickly washed his hands and dried them off on the paper towels she had waiting for him.

"Famished, are we?" She arched an eyebrow at him. Those twin dimples of hers appeared as she smiled. When she'd first arrived at the ranch, she'd immediately blended in as if she had been running it for years. She'd taken Ridge and Draven in as if they were her kids. She had two daughters, and he and his brother were the sons she'd never had. She spoiled the two of them like she did her own.

When Ridge was in the Navy, Bee had mailed care packages. She never wanted him to feel forgotten while he was stationed around the world. Many of his fellow crew had been jealous of the snacks he'd received, and when he'd been stateside, she'd send freshly baked goods that were always appreciated. She was a good woman, and he couldn't even imagine the ranch without her.

"I feel like I haven't eaten in three days." He chucked the paper towels in the trash before heading over to the coffee pot.

"Boy, have a seat. I'll bring everything to you." She gently pushed him toward the table. The woman didn't like having anyone in her space.

He held up his hands and backed away. He didn't want to be a victim of her towel. She was deadly with towel snapping.

"I know how you take your coffee. Been making it for years." She turned away, muttering.

He chuckled and took a seat across from Buck.

"Gotta lot of calls today?" Andy finished off the rest of his coffee and set his mug down.

The elder Harvey man shared the same blue eyes as his boys. Ridge took his father in, and it was like looking at his future self. His hair had once been dark like his sons' but was now completely gray.

"Not quite sure. I'm going to run into the clinic first. I'll make my rounds then I'm going to come back here. I believe we need to do some vaccines today." Ridge sat back as Bee arrived.

She set a steamy mug of black coffee in front of him along with his plate. His mouth watered at the sight of two large biscuits, home fries, sausage, bacon, and buttery grits. She'd even had his grits doctored just the way he liked them with cheese.

"Ms. Bee. You sure outdid yourself this morning."

"Well, I need to make sure you all have your strength." She walked away and snagged the carafe and came back to the table.

"Strength? You're trying to fatten us up," Ridge teased.

He reached for the jam sitting on the table. She filled Buck's mug up and moved over to Andy. Ridge didn't miss the way Andy's eyes tracked Bee or the way her hand rested on his shoulder while she poured him another cup of coffee.

"Like you have worries about getting fat." Bee gave an unladylike snort.

She went back over to return the carafe, and again, Andy tracked her.

Something was going on between them, but Ridge was not going to ask at the moment. His father should come clean. But he'd picked up on the two of them years ago. He didn't have anything against them being together. They were good for each other.

He made a mental note to say something to the old man...he should make an honest woman of Bee.

Ridge bit back a grin. He dove into his food and groaned. The woman definitely should not be single with cooking this good. Bee brought her own plate down and sat next to Ridge.

"Ms. Bee, it's because of your cooking that I make sure I keep up my workouts." Ridge grinned.

She smiled and waved him off, eating her food. He'd leave her alone for now so she could enjoy it. He was sure she had a busy day ahead of her.

Andy and Buck talked about the plan for the day and what was needed. Ridge half listened. He had his own day ahead of him that he needed to get together. Once he was done here, he'd stop by the clinic, grab his schedule, and pick up Heath, his tech, and they'd head out and start doing the ranch and farm calls.

"The new hands are working out pretty good," Buck said.

Ridge reached for his coffee and took a sip. The Silver Creek Ranch was a healing ranch for military veterans who needed help getting on their feet. His father had purchased the property when Ridge was a few years old. It was all he'd known growing up. His father had poured his blood, sweat, and tears into it to make it what it was today. Not only was it a thriving cattle ranch, but it had helped so many men and women.

"How many just started?" Ridge had cleared his plate, and according to his watch he had a couple more minutes until he had to leave.

"There's four who started about two weeks ago." Andy gave a nod toward Buck. "I'd have to agree. This group came to work. Not to say that others don't, but this group is certainly special. They have all jumped right into everything we offer here."

"That's good." Ridge certainly appreciated everything the ranch had to offer.

He and Draven had spent much time working alongside the men and women who came to Silver Creek. When he'd come of age, his father had escorted him down to the recruitment office. Andy hadn't voiced any objection that neither of his boys had followed behind him and gone into the Army.

Ridge had never once regretted entering the Navy. It was there he had met some of his longtime friends and comrades. He hadn't planned to stay long, just for a while then further his education. When he was a youngster, he'd dreamed of becoming a veterinarian. Lots of children always voiced it, but Ridge knew alongside serving his country that he wanted to help animals.

His time in the Navy hadn't been easy. He'd trained hard and went on multiple deployments. What he'd seen during his time abroad had changed something in him. His eyes had been opened to the way of the world. He'd come home a changed man. Once he'd got his papers, he'd enrolled into veterinary school and went on with his life.

The scars from his past were still there, but thanks to plenty of counseling and therapy, he'd learned to live life to the fullest.

He glanced around at the table and felt the love amongst everyone here. Little did they know they each had a role in making him the man he was today. They were what grounded him, helped him see there were good people worth loving and fighting for.

"If you have a chance, I want you to come check out the new bull we're getting. He should be here today," Andy said.

"Sure. Just text me when he arrives. I'll look him over before you let him out to the ladies." Ridge chuckled.

Andy always wanted a second opinion on the bulls they chose to stud the heifers. Not that Ridge expected to find anything different than what was shared with them about the bull, but it never hurt to give his approval to his father. Andy respected Ridge's opinion when it came to the animals.

Ridge glanced at his watch and saw the time. He pushed back and grabbed his dishes. "I better go. Ms. Bee, breakfast was amazing. Someone is going to make an honest woman out of you some day."

Andy coughed, choking on his sip of coffee. He gave a few more coughs before taking a long drag from his mug. That was all Ridge needed as confirmation that something was brewing between Andy and Bee. Ridge grinned and winked at her.

"Boy, hush up." Bee smiled bashfully. Her gaze flicked to Andy first before she lowered it to her plate. She picked at the remaining food and muttered something he couldn't catch.

"I'm just saying." Ridge couldn't help but tease her and his father indirectly. He moved over to the sink and rinsed off his plate and mug.

"Just leave the dishes in the sink. I'll load the dishwasher." Bee had a way about everything when it came to her kitchen. He'd tried to help once and loaded the dishwasher—and according to Bee, he'd done it wrong. The woman had taken everything out and reloaded it her way.

"Yes, ma'am." He placed them in the sink then

went and grabbed a travel mug and filled it with coffee to take it with him. He had a feeling he was going to need plenty of caffeine for today. Once he was done, he gave them a wave and left the house.

He got into his truck and shut the door. He pulled his cellphone out of his pocket and saw all of the missed messages from the office. Today was going to be a long day. He started the engine, turned the vehicle around, and drove down the main road. More house calls had been added last minute, and they were all deemed urgent.

Ridge tightened his grip on the steering wheel. He loved what he did and wouldn't change anything about it. He was needed in another sense. His days of serving his country may be over, but now he served in another way. Helping his community and the animals who depended on him.

Chapter Three

"Daisy, how are you doing tonight?" Melah leaned against the stall door and stared at her faithful horse. She had been worried about her gorgeous American Paint when she'd realized Daisy hadn't been eating her normal amount of food and she appeared to have a limp. Daisy's ears flickered as she stood off in the corner of her stall.

Daisy's brown and white colors were what had first captured Melah's attention. She had been in the market for a horse a few years ago. There had been a farm close to Melah's father's home that was looking on adopting out their horses. The owners were getting up in age and wanted to downsize on the number of animals they looked after. Melah had just happened to be home visiting when she'd heard. She and Daisy had hit it off immediately. It was love at first sight.

Her father, Vernon, had helped find a local family who would be able to board Daisy while Melah was gone. It had worked out perfectly for her over the years.

And now that Melah was out of the service, she'd need to start working on a forever home for her and Daisy. It was a bonus that she was able to bring Daisy with her to the Silver Creek Ranch. Daisy had been thriving there until recently.

Daisy turned and took a step toward her with a more pronounced limp.

"No," Melah whispered. She opened the door and flew inside. She bit her lip to keep her emotions from overtaking her. She didn't know what she'd do if she lost Daisy. She made her way to her and ran a hand along her neck. "Tell me you're going to be okay."

She snuck out a carrot she had put into her pocket to hide it from Daisy. Her horse was like her, she never turned down a snack. Melah held the carrot out to Daisy who sniffed it at first then turned her head away. Melah's eyes widened.

Carrots were one of Daisy's favorite snacks.

Melah tried to clear the lump in her throat. As if sensing her emotional distress, Daisy leaned down and rested her head on Melah's shoulder. Melah wrapped her arms around Daisy and just held on to her.

"Besides Dad, you're all I have," Melah whispered. She tightened her hold on Daisy.

Earlier that day when she'd first noticed the limp, she'd spoken with Andy about the local vet so she could call and have Daisy checked out. He'd said the vet was his son, Ridge. He'd given her Ridge's number in case she needed it. She wasn't sure if this was a true emergency, but she didn't know if Daisy was suffering. She couldn't bear the thought that her horse was in pain. She pulled back from Daisy and gave her a smile.

"Let's call the doctor and see if he can come check you out."

It was getting late, and she hated to make the call at this time of night. Most decent people were in bed. She took her cellphone out of her pajama pants and walked over to the door. She set the carrot down and slid her finger along the screen of her phone to find the doctor's number in her contacts.

She had planned to turn into bed but wanted to check in on Daisy first. There was no way she could go to sleep while Daisy could be out here fighting for her life. She found the number and tapped on it. The sound of ringing was cut short immediately.

"Hello?" a baritone voice answered.

Melah froze in place with her tongue stuck to the roof of her mouth. His voice sent a shiver down her spine. She swallowed hard, trying to get her words to form. Whoever this doctor was sounded tired as if he were tucked into bed with his woman. She closed her eyes and exhaled.

"Hi. Is this Dr. Harvey?" Her gaze locked in on Daisy who slowly limped toward her. Melah straightened to her full height. She didn't know where this slight bout of weakness was coming from, but she was not going to allow it to rule her. She was a tough chick. She'd survived deployments, harassment, and worse. She was stronger than this. Daisy depended on her.

"This is," he drawled.

Lord, the man's voice was rich and smooth. He could probably convince a whale to buy water.

"I'm so sorry to be calling at this hour. My horse, Daisy, I don't know what's wrong with her. She started limping and won't eat her snacks. She loves carrots and won't even bite—"

"Slow down, ma'am. It's going to be all right," Dr. Harvey interjected. "Just breathe."

Melah inhaled and blew out slowly. Her gaze trailed Daisy as she took another step.

"I'm sorry."

"No need to apologize. Now let's start with your name and where you are," he said calmly.

Melah blinked and groaned internally.

"My name is Melah. I just came on at Silver Creek as a hand a couple of weeks ago." She reached out a hand, rested it on Daisy's shoulder, and gave her a slow rub.

Daisy's large head swung her way and came to rest on her shoulder again.

"You're in the barn now?"

"Yes, sir." She eyed Daisy and sent up a prayer that this wasn't life-threatening. What could have happened to Daisy to cause this? Was it something she had done? Had she not paid attention to her enough when she took her out on the ranch? Did she get bitten?

Her heart raced with all of the possibilities of what could be wrong.

"I just got back on the ranch. I'll be there in less than three minutes. Just hang tight," he said.

She didn't know why, but for some strange reason, she believed him. The line went dead. She slid her phone back into her pocket. Daisy chose that moment to try to bite her bonnet off her head.

"Hey, that's mine. Leave it alone." Melah chuckled. She straightened up her cap and rubbed Daisy on her neck. She tilted her head back so she could watch Daisy. Well, at least her horse still had her humor. She didn't like when Melah wore things on her head. She always tried her best to take them off. Melah drummed up a smile and increased the pressure of her nails. The horse loved a good scratching, and at the moment she was enjoying Melah's attention. "Is this all you needed? Some attention?"

Daisy's soft neigh escaped her.

Many times Melah had found herself in tight situations, deployed, a gun in her face, even the situation with her sergeant, but she'd never felt so damn scared in her life that night. She shuddered at the memory, pushed it away, not wanting to relive the assault.

"How about this. You promise me that you are okay, and I will take you somewhere with wide-open spaces where you can graze as long as you like. There will be plenty of grass for you, a warm sun, trees with lots of shade. There will be a big lake where I can relax and fish, and we can just have a good old trip." Melah was not above bribing her horse. If that was what she had to do to make sure Daisy would pull through whatever this was, she'd do it. "How does that sound? There will be sun, all the apples and carrots we can buy. I'll even sneak you some of those donuts you like, even though you shouldn't be eating them."

"I don't know about her, but that sounds pretty damn good to me," a voice said behind her.

Melah spun around, reaching for her weapon that was not there. Her gaze locked on the figure leaning against the stall door, and she froze. His dark wavy hair stood up every which way as if he'd been combing his fingers through it. His blue eyes held a twinkle in them, but she could easily see the man was dead on his feet. His dark t-shirt and jeans had seen better days. She wasn't sure what they were caked in—better yet, she didn't want to know.

Her breath caught in her throat. This had to be the vet. She had thought his voice was something else—the man probably had to fight through droves of women daily.

"Melah, I take it?" He arched an eyebrow and tilted his head.

She jerked out a nod, unable to speak. She immediately wished she'd thrown on something other than her pjs when she'd come out to the barn.

She was currently done with members of the male species, but that didn't mean she couldn't appreciate this one in front of her.

"And who might we have here?"

"Daisy." Melah didn't miss the way his gaze ran over her. A shiver rippled through her. She'd guess it was only fair since she had just ogled him.

She stood straighter as he walked inside the stall. Suddenly the space seemed crowded.

"Um, thanks for coming so fast. I was worried about her."

"I could hear it in your voice." His lips curled up slightly in the corner.

Daisy hadn't taken her eyes off the doctor since the second he'd appeared. He held out a hand to allow her to get a whiff of him. Melah almost found herself inhaling, too. She blinked and took a step back. What the hell was wrong with her? It wasn't like she hadn't been around handsome men before, and at the moment she was not looking for a man.

Her ex-fiancé had made sure of that.

Melah didn't want to think of Pierce. When she'd needed him the most, he'd backed away from her and believed all of the lies that had been spread about her. That betrayal cut her profoundly. Five years they had been together. They had planned a life, spoke of children and growing old together.

All of that was now gone because he'd taken the easy road and decided he couldn't be with her if—

Not tonight. She wasn't going to go down that long road of sorrow and pain. She had enough to worry about at the moment. Daisy was her focus.

She blinked. Daisy tried to take a step toward Ridge—Dr. Harvey. Melah didn't say a word as she watched the two of them. Her horse was friendly, but she always checked people out first before warming up to them. Melah didn't blame her one bit. They were similar in nature, and it was no wonder they got along so well.

"Well, I see why you called." Ridge frowned slightly as he took a step back to force Daisy to take another step. His gaze was locked on her front leg.

"She's going to be okay, right? She's not going to —" Melah couldn't finish the sentence. She bit her lip and stared at the vet.

"Of course she'll be fine." Dr. Harvey swung his blue eyes to her.

Melah inhaled sharply. She hadn't realized he'd backed up far enough to where he was standing next to her. Daisy accomplished her goal and made it to Ridge. She sniffed the top of his hair, eliciting a hearty laugh from him.

"Daisy. Down, girl." Melah couldn't believe how her horse was acting. She'd only been in the doctor's presence for a few minutes and already she was sniffing him.

"Why, it's all right," Dr. Harvey drawled. He reached up and gave Daisy a good rubbing in between her eyes. Daisy closed her eyes and leaned into his touch.

Melah had to admit, she was quite jealous of her horse. She couldn't think of the last time she'd had attention from a member of the opposite sex. Much less have one of them rub on her—with her consent.

"Are you sure?" Melah couldn't help but ask. Daisy was her baby, and she was responsible for her. She didn't care how much it cost, he needed to save her. She didn't have much but she'd figure out a way.

"Well, I need to look at her hoof. See what's going on. I'm suspecting an infection. Let me grab my bag." He gave Daisy a good solid pat on the side of her neck and jogged over to the door where he'd left a large worn leather bag on the floor.

Melah moved over to Daisy and rubbed her

shoulder and neck. "Dr. Harvey said you should be fine. We'll get through this, girl."

Daisy head butted her gently and released a soft neigh.

"It's Ridge. You can call me Ridge. No need to be formal." He walked back to her and Daisy, this time with a few tools in his hands.

Melah tilted her head back so she could meet his gaze.

"But you are a doctor, right?" she said haughtily. She wasn't sure where this was coming from. It had been forever and a day since the last time she'd even attempted to flirt with someone. Again, not that she was looking for a man, but for some reason she felt relaxed around him. "I called you to come see about my horse."

"That I am, but again, you can call me Ridge. Unless you want me to call you by your title?"

"It's Corporal Battle, if you want to use it. But I'm a civilian now, so Miss Battle will do." She folded her arms and met his gaze head-on. "But if you insist that I call you by your first name, then I guess I can, Ridge."

"I insist." His eyes crinkled in the corner as he smiled. He jerked his head toward Daisy. "I'll need a little help. Think you can distract her?"

"Sure. She's usually good when she's getting her shoes done," Melah said.

Ridge positioned himself to hold Daisy's leg between his while he assessed her hoof. Melah watched how gentle he was with her.

"When was the last time she saw a farrier?" he asked.

"About a couple months ago. I was going to see about setting her up with the one who comes here." Melah winced at the sight of Daisy jerking her leg back.

"My bad, girl. I see the problem." He prodded her hoof, and she tried to jerk away again.

Melah continued to rub Daisy on her neck while she spoke softly to her as the doctor worked.

"It's definitely an infection. I'm just going to clean it out, then we'll need to put an antibacterial ointment on it. We'll need to keep this dry and clean so she can heal."

"But she'll be okay?"

"Oh yeah. Daisy girl is strong. I'll show you what to do, and she'll be right in no time. She's limping because she's in pain. I'll give you something for that tonight. By tomorrow she should be pain-free."

A foul smell reached Melah. She glanced down

at Ridge expelling some drainage from a wound on Daisy's hoof.

"Was it something I did? Or missed?" Melah felt horrible that Daisy was going through this. She racked her brain on what she could have done to prevent this.

"Nah, it happens sometimes. She's going to need some good loving care. Make sure she gets in with Mike. He's good. I'll take a look at her other hooves to make sure she's okay, but let's get this one dressed up to keep it clean and dry." He motioned to his bag and asked her to bring it over to him.

She became his assistant, handing him the items he needed to place a clean dressing around Daisy's leg. She didn't mind. It kept her busy instead of standing back and worrying. They worked well together to take care of Daisy.

"Let's wrap her up. Hand me that white roll right there."

Melah shifted things around in the bag where she knelt until she found what he'd described. She pulled it out and opened the plastic package, then placed it in his waiting hand. His fingers closed around hers. She gasped, an electric current zipping along her arm. She snatched her arm back and fell onto her butt. Her pulsed raced, and warmth filled her face.

"You all right, darling?" Ridge arched an eyebrow. His blue eyes twinkled as he took her in. He went back to work wrapping Daisy's leg and hoof. But it wasn't before his lips curled up in the corner.

"Yeah. I'm good." Melah closed her eyes for a moment, truly embarrassed. She pushed up from where she'd landed. Her knees were weak when she stood. She brushed off the debris from her pants and tried to get herself under control. Ridge was taking care of Daisy. That was all that mattered.

The way he made her heart race didn't mean anything.

Or the way he appeared to see right through her.

The confident way he carried himself, or how he was with her horse shouldn't have her wondering what he'd look like without the t-shirt, or what it would feel like to have his large hands running along her naked skin.

She blinked and inhaled sharply. She wasn't on the ranch to find a man. She was here to work. Find herself. Figure out what the next stage in her life would include.

Not to lust over the sexy veterinarian.

But daydreaming and lusting after a person wouldn't get her in trouble. She could dream, right?

"And we are done," Ridge announced. He allowed Daisy's leg to drop down. He stood to his full height and stretched out his back.

Melah's gaze dipped down to his stomach where his shirt was drawn tightly from him stretching. It molded to the ridges of his abdomen. The air escaped her. She tore her gaze from him and watched Daisy test out her hoof.

"I'll check back on her in a day or two to make sure everything is good. You'll have to make sure her dressing stays on so the wound can remain clean and dry."

Melah blinked. She had to focus on what he was saying so she'd be able to remember come morning.

Dressing needed to be changed. Hoof needed to stay dry and clean. Medicated ointment.

Got it.

"Thank you so much." Melah moved over to Daisy and rubbed her shoulder and neck. Daisy blew out a breath and butted Melah's hand with her head. Melah grinned at the move. She knew what that meant. She raced over to where she'd left the carrot and came back. She offered it to Daisy who promptly ate it in two bites.

"It was my pleasure." Ridge bent down and threw the items on the floor back in his bag. He zipped it shut and picked it up.

"That's my girl." Melah breathed a sigh of relief. She turned back to him and offered a smile. "I really appreciate you coming this late."

"I've been out practically all day. This is actually my first time getting back to the ranch since I left this morning." He combed his fingers through his hair then motioned to the door. "I can walk you out."

Any other day Melah would have insisted she could take care of herself. Which she could, but she figured he was just being nice. She gave a nod and wrapped her arms around Daisy one last time.

"I'll see you in the morning before I go to work. Get some rest." She took a step back and gave Daisy another smile before she spun on her heels.

They exited the stall and closed it. Melah paused by the door and sighed.

"She'll be fine. I promise," Ridge said.

"She just means so much to me. It's like having a kid." Melah smiled bashfully and pushed away from the door.

They strolled through the large barn toward the exit. It was dark and quiet outside. A pickup truck was parked near the barn doors.

"I get it, and that's what makes you a good mom to Daisy. You care."

It felt good to have someone realize how much she loved Daisy and not make fun of her for it. Pierce had never understood why she'd gone out and gotten a horse.

Why didn't you adopt a dog or a cat? His voice echoed in her head. She had spoken of her dream of owning a horse plenty of times. That had just showed her that he either didn't really listen to her or he hadn't thought she'd be capable of taking care of an animal like Daisy.

"It's just her and me. I was happy the ranch allowed me to bring my own horse. This was definitely a good move for me." She stared out at the open lands. The moon was high in the dark sky that was littered with twinkling stars. The ranch was stunning at night. She had spent plenty of time walking out here when the nightmares started. It wasn't often she could escape them, so she'd just walk or go for a run on the ranch. The fresh air helped her think.

"I'm glad you are here," he said.

She turned to him and found him watching her. "Oh?" She arched an eyebrow at him.

"This place is good for people like us. My father

had a dream of wanting to help soldiers, and this place does that. Whatever you need, they have it here."

"I'm learning that." She relaxed slightly. He was speaking in general about her being a soldier and coming to the ranch. Not him being happy that she was here. She doubted she'd see much of him after tonight. She'd been on the ranch for a couple of weeks now, and this was the first time she'd seen him. "Well, I'm thankful for your father and everything he has here. It's already helping."

"Good."

They fell into a comfortable silence as they both admired nature. Melah inhaled the fresh South Dakota air again and realized this was the most relaxed she had felt in a while.

"What do I owe you?" she asked. The thought just came to her. He was still the vet who had come to treat Daisy. There had to be a fee for it.

"No charge." He shook his head.

"Oh, no. I will pay you for your time. You are working." She folded her arms.

He may not know her, but he was going to learn really quick she didn't take handouts. She was going to reimburse him. He had just admitted he'd been working all day, and it was after midnight and he was just getting back on the ranch.

"I'm serious. No charge for Daisy. I just want to see her better." He hefted the bag up on his shoulder and motioned to his truck. "Are you staying in the bunkhouse? I can give you a ride."

"I am, but I prefer to walk. I do most nights, and don't try to change the subject. I will pay you for treating her."

"How about dinner?"

Melah's gaze flew to Ridge. Dinner? Was he asking her out on a date? She glanced down at herself and her now dirty jammy pants, t-shirt, and the flip-flops she'd tossed on. Seriously? Well, if he wasn't willing to take money, then she could at least buy the man a meal.

"As long as I'm paying." She tilted her head to the side.

His lips curled up into a wide grin.

"I can't remember the last time a woman treated me to a good meal." He laughed.

"Well, then you need to find a new woman." The words were out of her mouth before she could think. Her eyes widened as the realization set in.

Ridge burst out in a hefty laugh.

"I'm so sorry. That's not to say your wife is horrible or anything—"

"I'm not married." His smile faded.

His gaze swept her again, and when he met her eyes with his, her knees grew weaker. Something fluttered in her stomach.

"No girlfriend either."

It was as if he'd made a point to clarify he was unattached. Was he flirting with her? Or making a move? She had been out of the game way too long, so she wouldn't even know it unless a man plainly spelled it out for her.

"Oh." That was all she could muster. She swallowed hard and offered a small smile. "Well, you let me know when you are free and we can grab a bite to eat." She began walking away for fear of what else she may accidentally say. She gave a wave and spun on her heel and started on the path to the bunkhouse. She called out over her shoulder, "Goodnight."

"Sweet dreams, Melah."

A shiver rippled down her spine at the way he'd pronounced her name. She didn't dare turn around and look to see if he was watching her. She could feel the heat of his gaze on her. A silly smile graced her lips. She didn't know what had just happened, but she felt like a woman. Not one who had been assaulted, beaten down, or who had lost everything.

Just in those few moments, she'd felt like a new woman.

Like the one she could be once she'd finished healing.

Unable to resist, she held her head up higher and threw a little extra twist in her hips as she walked back to the house. Now that Daisy was okay, she could sleep.

And Melah had a funny feeling she knew who the star of her dreams would be tonight.

Chapter Four

"Don't worry about coming into the office. I can handle it. There's not much going on today," Faith said.

She was the other vet who worked with Ridge. The clinic had been owned by Dr. Turner who had been the local vet for almost fifty years. He had brought Ridge into the practice straight out of school. Ridge appreciated everything he had learned from the aging doctor. The moment Dr. Turner said he was ready to retire, Ridge had made him an offer for the clinic and purchased it.

Their office was busy, and he had needed help. One vet was not enough for this area, so he'd recruited Faith. He'd known her for years. They'd both grown up in Ironhaven. She was a few years younger than him. Her older sister had graduated high school with Ridge. The moment he'd called her with the offer, she'd accepted. It allowed her to have a shorter commute than before.

"You sure? I just want to shower really quick and then I can head in." He grimaced at the grime on him. He'd just come from one of the farm calls. A cow had a breech birth, and he'd had to assist to get the calf out. It was an intense delivery, but Momma and babe were doing well when he'd left. Birthing calves was not as glamorous as some made it out to be. His clothes were soaked in only God knew what.

"I'm positive. You've been out practically thirty-six hours. Clean up, sit down, and have a beer."

"That does sound good." Ridge laughed. He turned onto the main road of the ranch and picked up speed. He'd be home in mere minutes, but he wasn't going to be relaxing. If he wasn't going to go into the office, then he'd head out onto the ranch and jump in to help. His father and Buck could always use an extra hand.

"That's a doctor's order. I don't want to see you until tomorrow. I'll take over calls then, and you can be in the office. We have a list of cats who need to be spayed and neutered tomorrow on the books."

Ridge rolled his eyes. Not that he didn't like

working in the office, but being out on the road and on the farms and ranches was his first love. He enjoyed treating the big animals.

"Fine. See you in the morning." He chuckled.

Faith had a bossy side to her, and she'd literally remove him from the office by force if he showed up. They had become good friends, and he knew by her tone that she meant business. He disconnected the call.

Ridge guided his pickup home. He relaxed when he caught sight of the house he'd built from the ground up. Andy had gifted him and Draven a portion of land for them to build homes on. The Silver Creek Ranch was Andy's legacy, and he and Draven already knew they'd be taking over one day. Ranching was in their blood.

He hit the garage door opener and pulled into the garage once the door opened. He killed the engine and exhaled. It did feel damn good to be home. He probably should listen to Faith and relax, but he'd be kidding himself. He'd feel bad for at least not offering to help out on the ranch. He got out of the truck and slammed the door shut. He grabbed his duffle bag from the back and dragged it up on his shoulder. At the house, he hit the button on the wall to close the garage, kicked off his boots, then went inside the house.

He was a mess, and he'd be damned if he tracked dirt, blood, and birth into his house. The garage led into a mudroom where he stripped his clothes off. He grimaced at the sight of them. He should probably burn them, that's how bad they looked. He left the duffle bag by the door and stopped in the laundry room where he tossed the clothes in the washing machine. He started the cycle then went up to his bedroom.

It was mid-afternoon, and it had been a long day. Last night he had gotten a few hours of sleep before he'd been awakened by an emergency call for a goat. After that, he'd had back-to-back calls with the last being the breeched heifer.

He stripped off his underwear. In his en suite bathroom, he caught the reflection of himself.

"Shit."

He combed his fingers through his hair. He had darkened areas underneath his eyes, and he caught more gray hairs he hadn't seen before. He moved away from the mirror and turned the shower water on. He waited until steam billowed. His muscles were screaming at the moment, and the hot water had better work a miracle on him.

He stepped into the shower and groaned. The water felt damn good. He turned around to allow it to slide all over him. He stood underneath the spray to soak his hair. He felt dirty everywhere. He'd taken a shower last night when he'd got home, but at the moment he couldn't tell. Being a vet was a very dirty job. It was not all rainbows and sunshine.

He closed his eyes, the water beating into his muscles. He leaned forward and rested a hand on the wall while the water worked its magic.

Brown soulful eyes came to mind.

Melah. Battle.

The memory of her voice on the phone had done something to him. He could hear the urgency, the need, the attempt to hold her shit together because her horse was in trouble. Even if he had been in bed sleep, he'd have rushed to help her.

The moment he'd walked in and heard her trying to bribe her horse, he knew he'd do anything to ensure that damn animal would make it.

Not that Daisy was in trouble of leaving this earth. Melah had done what all good horse parents would do. She'd recognized something was wrong and sought help immediately. The infection had been caught early enough that he was confident Daisy would fully recover. He'd done a small incision in the wound, cleaned it out so it would heal properly. Daisy would be back to normal soon with no signs of the infection. Melah, he was sure, would do as he'd instructed. Before he'd left that morning, he'd dropped off supplies to the barn and left them outside Daisy's stall where Melah would see them.

Her eyes drew him to her. They were a rich brown and almond-shaped. Her smooth tawny skin appeared to be soft and supple. He'd had to keep his hands busy to not touch her. He'd immediately felt an attraction to her. It didn't matter that she was dressed for bed. That showed him how much she cared for her horse. She was apparently checking on Daisy before going to bed. Her falling on her butt while helping him had been too cute. He'd bitten back a joke that had hovered on his tongue when he'd seen her scramble to get up.

He lifted his head and reached for his washcloth and soap. He couldn't stand here all day reminiscing about the lovely woman he'd helped last night.

Which reminded him, he had to let her know when he'd be available to grab a bite to eat. He'd refused to allow her to pay him for treating Daisy. His clinic was booming and doing well. He didn't need her money. His only payment would be Daisy getting better and not limping.

But since she'd insisted—and he could see the woman held a stubborn streak to her—he'd made the offer of food.

Well, then you need to find a new woman.

She was a woman who apparently didn't have a filter, and he loved that. The horror that had crossed her face had him laughing. He guessed he had set himself up when he'd said that a woman had never treated him to a meal. It wasn't far from the truth. It had been a while since he'd been in a relationship. His last one ended on pretty good terms. They both realized they were wanting two different things in life. That had been about two years ago when him and Raquel split.

He'd dated since Raquel, but no one caught his eye to where he wanted something permanent with them. He wanted a partner in life. He aspired to getting married one day. He wasn't too old yet. At thirty-eight, he'd have hoped he'd be married by now and maybe have a kid or two. But apparently it wasn't in the cards yet.

Hell, Draven had a fiancée. Who would have thought his grouch of a brother would have put a ring on a woman's finger before him? That just proved that Ridge needed to be patient. Maybe his future wife would fall into his arms and the rest would be history.

He snorted at the thought.

Things like that didn't happen that easily for him. He scrubbed his entire body at least three times to ensure all of the blood and dirt was off him. He quickly washed his hair before shutting off the water. He grabbed his towel and ran it over his head.

A woman to come home to would be nice. This big house could get lonely, and he'd love to have someone to share this with. Someone who he could chill on the couch with, watch movies, spend time with, share their day with each other.

Soulful brown eyes came to mind.

He wrapped the towel around his waist and stepped out of the shower. He shouldn't be thinking of Melah. She was like all of the other soldiers who came through Silver Creek. She was here to get help and move on. How long she was on the ranch was up to her.

Those eyes of hers held stories. There was a darkness hiding in them. He was sure if she was here, it was for a reason. Even though she smiled, he could see she didn't do it often. Deep down, he wanted to see her do it more. Even if her time was short-lived here on the ranch, he wanted to be the one to help her smile more.

He strolled back into his room and snatched his phone off the nightstand. He swiped the screen and went into his contacts. When he found the name, he hit it and placed the call on speakerphone.

"Howdy, Ridge," Buck's gravelly voice came through the line.

"Where do you need me?" He held the phone as he walked over to his dresser to grab a pair of under-wear. It wouldn't take him long to get dressed and be out on the ranch.

"We're good—"

"Seriously, Buck. Don't bullshit me. You need another set of hands. I'm home for the day." Ridge set his phone down and slid on his boxer briefs. He pulled out another drawer and snagged a fresh t-shirt to throw on. It was quite warm outside today.

"Well, if you insist, then you can come and meet me out here in the eastern pasture. I want you to check out a couple of the cows," Buck said.

"I'll be there shortly." Ridge cut the call before Buck tried to talk him out of it. He finished getting dressed and headed back downstairs. He went into the kitchen and opened the fridge door to eye the contents. He grinned at the sight of a sandwich waiting for him.

Ms. Bee must have stopped by. He glanced around his kitchen. It sparkled. He shook his head and lifted the plate out of the fridge. He set it on the island and went back for a bottle of water and snagged a bag of chips out of his pantry.

What would they all do without Ms. Bee? He sure as hell didn't want to think about it. His father better stop farting around and claim his woman. They could hide it all they wanted, but it didn't take much to see what was between them. Ridge's gaze landed on the plate of cookies sitting on the counter, and he released a groan. They were his favorite. Chocolate chip. The woman must be an angel from Heaven. That was the only place a woman like her could be from.

"Hell, if Pops don't marry her, I just might." He sat and dragged the plate over to him. He downed the sandwich before finishing off the bag of chips. This was a much better lunch than what he'd have thrown together. He probably would have just eaten the bag of chips then headed out.

He figured he'd better enjoy sitting for a few more minutes before he left. He was still on call until the morning. There was no telling how the rest of the day would go. He reached for a cookie and took a bite.

Oh, yeah. He was going to sit here and enjoy these before he went out on the ranch.

* * *

"What's going on?" Ridge got out of the four-wheeler and headed over to where Buck stood near a gate. There was a herd of cows being moved inside the gates. He glanced around and nodded to the hands he knew. But there was one on a horse who caught his attention.

Melah.

She wasn't on Daisy. She was riding a different horse. He hadn't asked her if Daisy was a working horse. He hadn't even thought about it. His gaze remained on her and the graceful way she guided the horse and chased down a cow who was trying to be defiant. She and the horse moved as one. Melah hollered out and guided the horse in front of the cow and pushed it in the direction of the other cattle.

"We've been noticing some diarrhea from quite a few of the cows in this herd. I want you to check them out. Not sure if anything is going around that you may have heard of, but I figured it would be best to have you look them over to make sure," Buck said.

Ridge leaned against the gate and quickly assessed the cattle. Some looked a little thinner than they should be, but otherwise he didn't see anything alarming.

"Oh, no you don't. Get your ass in there with the rest," a feminine voice growled.

Ridge glanced back over and caught sight of Melah chasing down another cow who tried to make their escape from going inside with the rest. Her maneuverability on the horse was impressive. The cow didn't stand a chance against her. It was forced to get in line with the others and trotted inside the gated-off area.

"That's Melah. She recently joined us. Hard worker. Haven't seen anyone dive right into work like her in a while," Buck said. She and the others quickly got the rest of the herd inside the holding area. "Have you met her yet?"

"Actually, I have. She called about her horse last night," Ridge said.

"Oh?" Buck's eyebrows shot up high. "Is everything all right? I was wondering why she'd asked to borrow one of the ranch's."

"Yeah, she was limping, and Melah was worried

about her." He left out how worried and scared she'd been. She'd made the right call. He couldn't count all of the horse owners who waited until it was damn near too late to call about a lame horse. "Horse will be fine. She's letting her rest a bit."

Buck gave a nod.

The hands gathered on the other side of the gate and fell into a conversation. Ridge took in her t-shirt, jeans, and boots. Her wide-brimmed hat sat low and hid her face from him. He already had her beauty ingrained in his mind. He exhaled and remembered why Buck had said he'd brought him out here.

"When did you notice the first bout of diarrhea?" He tried to remember if he'd heard anything from the other farms. There were certain viral diseases that could be contagious, and the community of ranchers would alert each other to something like this. It was a good thing Buck was quarantining this herd. Until they knew what this was, they wouldn't want them to be around other cows. The last thing they'd need was for this to be something extremely contagious and deadly.

"A few days ago. I didn't think nothing of it, thinking maybe it was something the cows had eaten. I believe it was two at first before we noticed more having it. Trent alerted me which ones."

Buck pulled out a piece of paper from his pocket and handed it to Ridge. There were numbers listed that would line up to the cows. This was perfect. It would allow Ridge to know which cows to test first.

"I'll grab some samples and send them out to be tested. Let's see what comes back. In the meanwhile, keep them quarantined until I get the results back," Ridge announced.

"That's what I figured you'd say." Buck chuckled.

"What the hell you call me for then?" Ridge slapped Buck on the shoulder.

The lead hand came with years of experience. There wasn't a better man for this job. His father was lucky to have Buck on at the ranch.

"You know what to do."

"I ain't got no fancy degrees. I'll leave the science stuff up to you. I only know the basics." Buck shook his head. His weathered face crinkled in the corners by his eyes. He brought a toothpick out of his pocket and slipped it between his lips. The older cowboy had given up smoking years ago. He'd had a scare a while back with his lungs that had led him to be hospitalized. It only took one time where he couldn't breathe for him to give up cigarettes. "Plus, if I did all the work, what would there be for you to do, kid?"

Ridge barked a laugh and shook his head. He pushed off the gate and headed over to the vehicle he used to get around the ranch. In the back of it, he kept supplies he may need. One of the things he dreaded most was getting fresh stool samples from cattle. They could be ornery, and it could be dangerous if one didn't know what they were doing. He didn't have his vet tech, Heath, with him today, so he'd have to have the hands help him out.

He looked up, and his attention fell on Melah. She had taken off her hat and wiped her brow with the back of her arm. She turned and met his gaze. She paused for a moment then offered him a small smile. He nodded to her then grabbed the bag and walked back over to holding area.

This was about to get interesting.

Chapter Five

"I wouldn't want to be the doc right now." Trent chuckled.

Melah inhaled sharply at the mention of 'the doc'. She tried to keep her face free of emotions. She glanced over at the other hand and raised an eyebrow.

"Why?" She held reins of the horse she'd borrowed. Daisy was a working horse, but since she had the wound, Melah felt it was best to let her girl rest. She had found the material and medicated ointment Ridge had left for Daisy this morning when she'd checked on her. She'd change the dressing after work. It didn't appear to be hard to do, so she'd try her hand at it.

"He's going to need a stool sample." Ethan snorted.

They all sat on their horses, waiting around while Buck spoke with Ridge. Melah glanced back over at them. The moment Ridge threw his head back and laughed, that fluttering in her stomach returned. She didn't know what it was about a man who enjoyed life the way he did. She didn't know his story, only that he had been in the Navy, then had come home, went to school, and now he was the local veterinarian.

Oh, and he was single.

That is not important, she reminded herself.

Okay, how about he was extremely handsome. Fit. Had a good job.

Nope. Stop thinking of him like that, she scolded herself.

He was a nice guy who'd come out and treated her horse and wouldn't take payment. She swallowed hard, remembering that he'd take a meal as payment for treating Daisy. Why did her nerves act up at the thought of being alone with him at a restaurant? Maybe she could pick him up something to eat and drop it off at his house. That would still be her providing a meal for him.

It wasn't like she had a kitchen she could cook in.

She wasn't the best cook, but she had certain dishes she'd perfected. Pierce had loved when she'd cooked, because that man could not even boil water.

We are not thinking of Pierce right now either!

She sighed. It was official—she was going crazy.

Who spoke to themselves and responded? She was sure that was the definition of deranged.

"So should we go out and collect some of the poop that dropped from the cattle?" The moment the words fell from her lips, she knew it sounded dumb.

"That would only be too easy." Trent lifted his baseball cap and combed his fingers through his hair. He replaced the hat and motioned to Ridge walking toward his terrain vehicle. "He's going to want a fresh sample. Straight from the sources."

Melah's eyes widened. Well, she shouldn't be too surprised.

"I'm not sticking nothing in no cow's ass." Ethan snickered.

"I ain't either," Trent said.

Their gazes fell to her. She glanced at both of them. Ethan was new to the ranch, like her. He'd been there about two months and already fit in. When she'd first met him, she'd figured he'd been there much longer. Ethan was former Navy. He hadn't said much about this time in the service, but then again, neither had she. So far, he appeared to be a good guy. He'd helped her out a few times since she'd started.

"What y'all looking at me for? I'm not the doctor. He can collect his own samples," she scoffed.

The guys chuckled then assured her the doctor would be obtaining the samples but may need help. Melah relaxed slightly. She eyed the herd and wondered if he'd need samples from all of the cattle. There had to be about thirty to forty in this group.

"Howdy, y'all," Ridge called out as he approached with Buck strolling next to him. He carried his medical bag just like he had when he'd come to see Daisy.

Melah tried to keep her face neutral, but her damn heart was thinking otherwise. Her pulse spiked as he grew closer. Last night, she'd thought he'd been handsome. That had been in the low light of the barn, but now in the middle of the day with the sun providing ample light, her breath stalled in her chest.

His dark hair looked as if it had been recently raked with his fingers, and his blue eyes were bright and clear. His jeans and Silver Creek t-shirt had no business molding to him the way they did. What was it with a man in tight Wranglers?

Melah swallowed hard and took him in. She blinked when silence fell around her. She glanced around at the men who were all staring at her.

"I'm sorry. Did you say something?" Her cheeks grew warm. This had never happened to her before. Even out in the desert, when stressed with life-or-death situations, she was always focused on the mission at hand. She'd never blanked out before, lost in a daydream.

"We were asking who would feel the most comfortable assisting Ridge," Buck said.

Melah relaxed slightly. At least she hadn't missed anything too important.

"I could. What would you need me to do?" she asked.

Ridge began to instruct them on what was needed. He read off a short list of numbers which were the cows he'd start with. Trent and Ethan would corral the cows into the chutes that would hold the cow and keep them from hurting themselves and them. She'd be the one helping put the samples in the appropriate containers and making sure the labels matched the cows.

Simple enough.

Only there was nothing simple about obtaining samples from cattle who didn't understand what was going on. Trent and Ethan had to work hard to capture the correct cattle and force them into the chute.

Melah was extremely curious about the process. She watched how Ridge was with the animals. He had a plastic sleeve placed on his arm while he pushed instruments into the cow and collected the stool samples. Never in a million years would she have thought she'd be assisting a doctor taking shit out of an animal.

"Here you go." Ridge turned from the cow with the sample.

She wrinkled up her nose and held open the container. She'd already labeled it with the cow's corresponding number and the date.

"God, that stinks," she muttered.

"Well, it is cow shit." Ridge laughed.

She rolled her eyes and closed the container. She set it on the ground near his bag. She had tried to get a system together so it would be easier on them. She was all about working smarter and not harder.

"Don't tell me this is your first time smelling it up close."

"Of course not." She stood to her full height.

She was on the outside of the gate nearest Ridge. He was right inside with the cattle. Trent and Ethan were off trying to gather the next cow, while Buck had come in to help as well. He and Ridge worked together to free the first cow who ran free.

"That one I'm definitely a little worried about. She looks too thin." Ridge turned to Melah. "Can you write underweight next to 129. I want to make sure I remember which ones looks a bit sickly."

"Yes, sir." She turned back and grabbed the notepad she had found in his bag and decided to redo the list on the larger paper. Hopefully this would help him out to determine what was going on with the animals. She hoped it was nothing serious. She'd hate if anything happened to them. Melah wasn't too ashamed to admit she had a big heart when it came to animals.

Sometimes she preferred them to people.

At least these cows didn't understand what was happening to them and reacted off of fear and trying to protect themselves.

Humans, on the other hand—some could be downright cruel.

Images of Staff Sergeant Theo English came to mind. Tremors racked her hands as memories rushed to the forefront of her mind. His snarling face. His warm breath sliding along her cheek when she'd turned her face from him. His strong grip pinning her arms downs. The helplessness that filled her. The anger that she wasn't strong enough to get him off her. Even with all of her training, she'd still become a victim.

It should have never happened.

He had been her superior. Someone she'd taken orders from. Someone she was supposed to trust. He was an ass to not only her, but all the females of the unit. But for some strange reason he'd singled her out.

She inhaled sharply and tried to not relive that night. She'd completely be embarrassed if she lost her shit right here in front of the men. She was thankful she was kneeling and they couldn't see her face. The world swam before her. She blew out a deep breath and tried to utilize what she'd learned in therapy. Breathing exercises helped keep the panic attacks away. For the longest, she hadn't known what was wrong with her. She'd thought she was having a heart attack once and had even taken herself to a local emergency room. All of her testing came out negative. Her heart was in perfect shape. It wasn't until later that she was diagnosed with anxiety and panic attacks.

"You good, Battle?" Trent called out.

She jerked her head in a nod. Trent may not know what exactly had led her to start attending the therapy sessions, but she remembered his offer.

"Want to take a minute?"

"No. I'm good. I just got a little dizzy," she lied. She opened her eyes and pushed up off the ground. Her water canteen was in the saddlebags on Thunder, her borrowed horse. Thunder and the other horses were off grazing underneath a large, shaded tree. She turned and found Trent watching her with a knowing expression.

"You need a break?" Ridge asked.

"I can go get you some water—" Buck offered.

She shook her head. "No, I'm fine. It's just the heat. I probably haven't drunk as much as I should. I'm fine. I promise," she assured them.

She didn't want to come off as if she couldn't hold her own with them. This was a momentary lapse, and she'd get through it. She inhaled and offered a small smile. She snagged the next container and walked over to the gate. Ridge's gaze swept her again. There was something in his eyes she couldn't read. As if satisfied with what he saw, he turned to the chute.

Trent and Ethan worked on bringing the next

cow over for its sample. They all worked together, and pretty soon they had gathered all the samples from the targets from the list and a few extra. Ridge was very thorough when it came to his job. Melah made sure that everything was properly labeled, and she even had notes from comments Ridge had spoken jotted down on the notepad.

Ridge's job actually had her interest piqued. She hadn't thought too much about what career she'd try to enter now she was out of the service. She'd thought about moving back home with her father and enrolling in school. It would be completely paid for by the government. She knew plenty of soldiers who'd obtained their degrees either before entering the service or while they were serving. Melah had taken a few classes online while enlisted, but she hadn't truly found something that held her attention.

"Thanks for the help. This went much faster than I thought it would," Ridge announced.

"Not a problem, as long as you were the one doing the shit collecting." Trent moved toward Ethan and jerked his head at the empty troughs. "Let's get them fed and watered before we leave."

Melah figured she'd help the guys. She looked down at her watch. It was almost time for her to get off work. She'd been up and out on the ranch before dawn. She hadn't gotten much sleep. Not that she needed much.

"How long until you get the results back?" Buck asked.

"Should be a few days. I'll make it an urgent request so we can know for sure. If it's something contagious, we'll have to alert the neighboring ranches," Ridge said.

"I know." Buck nodded.

"What would be the best-case scenario?" Melah got to thinking that it wasn't uncommon to have diarrhea here and there. Everyone had it once in a while. She'd hate to think that everyone would go see a doctor with each bout. What if the cows had some bad feed? Or tainted water? Or ate each other's shit, because she'd seen that before.

"If it had to be anything, I'm hoping not contagious, and something that could be treated with a simple round of antibiotics. If that's the case, we'll treat the entire herd to make sure they're all good," Ridge said.

"And worse-case?" she asked.

"The entire herd comes down with a deadly disease that will wipe them all out," he replied grimly.

Silence fell between them. Melah hoped the

cattle would be okay. She may not know the business side of a cattle ranch, but she could imagine an entire herd dying from a disease would be costly for Andy.

"Thanks for coming out again, Ridge. I better go. The day's not quite over for me yet." Buck nodded to her and Ridge then walked toward his horse.

Melah moved over to the gate and leaned her arms on it. The sounds of the cow grunts and moos filled the air. Trent and Ethan went around and ensured the water was filled to the brim and the food barrels were full.

Ridge came to stand by her without a word. The sun was still high. The warmth beat down on her. She needed a hot shower. A trail of sweat slid down the center of her back. She tried to not look over at Ridge, but her body was responding to him standing so close to her. She tried to will her heart rate to slow down. How was the man pushing instruments into a cow one moment, then able to still smell so damn good?

"How did you know you wanted to be a vet?" She peeked over at him and found his attention off in the distance. The Silver Creek Ranch was an alluring spread with ample rolling hills and flat land. She'd already explored it several times with Daisy and hadn't found a spot that wasn't appealing. He and his brother had been lucky growing up here.

She, on the other hand, had moved around with her father her entire childhood from base to base. Some were here in the States while others were abroad. She valued her time with her father, but it would have been nice to have a steady home when she was a kid. She had gotten used to moving and having to start over with making new friends. The only steady home she had known was her uncle and aunt's house. It wasn't until she was seventeen that her father had purchased his first home near his brother.

Her Uncle Billy and Aunt Sherrie were her second set of parents. When her father was deployed, she'd go and stay with them. There were times he'd been deployed for three to six months, and the longest time she could remember was around eighteen months. Billy and Sherrie were a blessing. They had opened up their home to her. Their daughter, Athena, was the best cousin and friend a girl could have.

Athena was one year older than Melah. They'd grown up like sisters. She missed Athena something fierce, and now that she'd thought of her, she made a mental note to call her.

"I've known since I was a kid." Ridge glanced down at his hands at first before looking over at her. "I guess I could say I'm lucky. I wanted to serve my country then I wanted to take care of animals. I've gotten to do both."

"I can tell you really like what you do," she said softly. She found herself getting lost in his piercing blue eyes. They reminded her of a clear sky. Her gaze dropped down to his mouth, and that was a dangerous move. She swallowed hard and shifted her gaze down. She didn't even want to think about his lips on hers or placed anywhere on her body.

"I do. Animals are helpless and depend on us. When they are sick, they need someone to take care of them, or if they need help giving birth, I'm happy to help as well."

"But when things go wrong, then what?" She brought her eyes back up to his face.

He was staring out at the cattle. She was sure his job wasn't easy. Even she knew things went wrong with animals who were sick. As much as she had freaked out about Daisy, she was sure some other horse mom wasn't as lucky.

"Then I want to be there for them still to ensure they pass as humanely as possible," he said.

"Do you lose patients often?" She rested her

cheek in her palm. She was truly fascinated with not only the man before her, but with what he did for a living. Not only had he accomplished one goal in life, but he was also fulfilling another one.

While here she was, trying to figure out her second phase in life. She'd honestly thought she'd have stayed in the Army much longer. She'd dreamed of going up in rank, but since accusing her staff sergeant of sexual assault, all of that was ruined. Even though he'd been found guilty, she, the victim, had suffered even more.

She'd heard plenty of times that she should have kept her mouth shut. That she could have transferred out. What really pissed her off were those who'd tried to say she was the one who'd instigated the entire scheme.

That cut her deep.

What drove home the knife in her heart was that Pierce, the man she had been set to marry, believed she was having an affair with Theo and she'd got caught.

She swallowed hard and blinked a few times.

Her hand curled up in a fist as the memory of that argument surfaced.

"Are you shitting me?" she screamed.

"You're gone all the time. I go days, maybe even

weeks without hearing from you. If I'm the man you love, then why is that?" Pierce folded his arms.

Her mouth dropped open at his accusation.

"What don't you get about being deployed? I was in the fucking desert. Enemy territory. Guns getting shoved in my face, and you are worried about me cheating on you?" She had been deployed for six months and had recently come home. When she should be getting comfort from her man after she'd officially filed her complaint against Theo, this was what she was met with.

"It happens all the time," he snarled.

"Do you even know me? You know I've been faithful to you."

"How do I?"

Melah blinked and shook off the memory. Pierce was a piece of shit. His true colors had come out that day, and she was so thankful she'd seen them then. It had hurt to have the man—one she'd thought loved her—abandon her almost immediately when things got tough.

According to Athena, she'd dodged a bullet.

"More than I like," he murmured.

Melah couldn't help but feel her heart tug at the sound of Ridge's voice. There was a pure sadness in the tone. He deserved to go out and be treated with a good meal. It was the least she could do for him for looking after Daisy. Dropping food off to him wouldn't do. She turned to him and drew up her big girl panties.

"Are you available for a bite to eat tonight? I don't want you to think I forgot about paying you for your trouble last night."

He smirked and glanced over at her. Those blue eyes of his captured her again. That fluttering in her stomach reappeared. She'd never experienced this sensation before. There was something about Ridge.

This was not going to be a date.

It's payment.

Keep your focus, woman.

"I am available."

"Well, you pick out the place and I'll treat." She stood to her full height, which didn't do much. She was five foot six, and standing next to Ridge made her appear to be much shorter. He had to be about six one or two. She didn't think she'd ever taken a man out to eat before. Grabbing food in the barracks didn't count when it was her and friends.

Again, this was not a date. This would be no different than her going out to grab a bite to eat with her friend, Issac. That goofball never let her pay. Even when it was his birthday and they had met up in his hometown of Dallas last year, he'd refused to allow her to open her purse.

"Mind if I drive?" Ridge arched an eyebrow at her while that devilish smile of his lingered.

She squeezed her legs together. Her core clenched at the heat that appeared in his gaze as it swept over her again. She may be getting in over her head with this one.

One dinner. That was it. She could handle this. Maybe they could even become friends. She hadn't come here to hook up with anyone, but developing a friendship with others on the ranch wasn't a bad idea.

"I guess I could let you." She shrugged. She was still learning the town, so it would probably be best he did drive.

"Be ready at six." He pushed off the gate and snagged his bag from the ground.

He ambled away from her, and she couldn't tear her eyes off his ass if she tried.

Damn Wranglers and how well they looked on sexy cowboys.

She was sure they were the death of women everywhere.

Chapter Six

Ridge was running a little behind, but he'd still be on time for picking up Melah. He'd run the stool samples to the clinic so they could be sent out. He didn't feel like keeping cow dung in his fridge until the morning, so he drove up to the clinic. It wouldn't have been the first time he'd done it but he truly wanted to get the samples processed because it was important.

He stepped out of his house and shut the door behind him. Being a vet was not for the weary. After a few hours of playing in cow shit, he'd needed another shower. He jogged down the steps to his pickup truck. He slid into it and hit the start button. The engine roared to life. He threw the vehicle into reverse and turned it around.

The drive to the women's bunkhouse wouldn't take him long. He glanced over at the time on the truck's computer screen: fifteen minutes to spare. He tightened his grip on the steering wheel. He didn't know why, but he was anxious to see Melah again.

Her questions earlier about his career choices touched him. It allowed him to think of all the hard work he'd had to put in to get to where he was today. Not many had a story like he did. There were so many men and women who came out of the military lost and broken with no options in life.

He'd trained hard in the Navy and given his all. When he'd received his discharge papers, he'd been excited to go home so he could start veterinarian school where he'd had to train just as hard as in the Navy. He'd graduated at the top of his class. He'd even had luck in obtaining a job before he'd finished school, thanks to Dr. Turner. Not a day went by where he wasn't thankful for all the opportunities he'd had in life.

That was why the Silver Creek Ranch was so important to his family. They may not be able to help all of the soldiers who came home lost and broken, but those they had were changed for the better. Ridge ensured he worked side by side with the men and women who came to the ranch.

The house came into view. There were cars and trucks parked in the lot near it. Not all of the hands stayed on the ranch. Most found rented housing in town. He drove up to the house and parked near the door. It was an old barn his father had converted years ago.

He shut the engine off and got out of the truck. The door opened, and Aimee stepped out.

"Hey, Aimee. How are you?" He ambled over to where she stood. There was only a couple of stairs and the doorway.

"I'm good. I hear you are getting Melah off the ranch."

She attempted a smile, but it didn't reach her eyes. He stiffened at the warning that burned bright in them.

"Yeah. She was trying to pay me for coming to see her horse last night." He stopped a few feet away from her.

He read the warning loud and clear. She'd been here for a short while, and he'd spoken with her several times. She was definitely a momma bear type person, and her hackles were raised.

"She kept insisting, so I told her she could just buy me something to eat."

"So this is payment for Daisy and nothing else?" She arched an eyebrow at him.

He frowned at her expression. What was she trying to hint at?

"Nothing else." He raised his hands to show his palms.

She studied him for a minute, giving him a nod. She glanced over at the door then glanced back his way.

"Listen, I don't know much about her, but she's been through some things. She has nightmares. Bad ones. The woman barely sleeps. Just be careful with her."

Ridge ran a hand along his face. He hated to think that something had happened to Melah. Even though he couldn't say he was surprised. Most of the soldiers who came here had interesting backgrounds to say the least. He remembered how she'd acted when he'd startled her in the barn. Had she had a weapon on her, she definitely would have pulled a gun on him.

"I hear you, Aimee. We are just grabbing a bite to eat. Nothing else," he repeated.

The door opened, and Melah exited the house. The air inside Ridge's lungs escaped him as if someone had slammed something against his stomach.

He'd thought she had been beautiful in her jammies and the silk cap that had covered her head last night, or earlier that day when she was riding the horse wrangling cattle.

This Melah was a fucking knockout.

Her dark hair was left hanging down with soft curls on the ends. She had even put on light makeup and gloss on her lips. She was dressed in a soft cream shirt, jeans that looked as if she had to be poured into them, and sandals.

"Hey, guys." Melah glanced between them with a curious expression. "Everything good out here?"

"Yeah, of course. I was out here busting Ridge's balls. Giving him the ol' 'we girls stick together so he better be a gentleman' chat." Aimee grinned, and again, the smile didn't reach her eyes.

Ridge heard the warning again. She was Air Force, and he didn't want to get on her bad side. He appreciated how Aimee was willing to stick up for Melah, but he was the last person who'd try to harm her.

"I'll be fine. This is just grabbing something to eat. I haven't really explored the town much, so it would be nice to know where there's good food when I don't want to eat here on the ranch."

"And not eat Ms. Bee's cooking?" Aimee gasped.

"You know what I mean. That woman has to take a break sometime." Melah chuckled. She draped her purse strap on her shoulder and came down to stand next to him. She tilted her head back and smiled. "Are you ready for me to treat you?"

"Yes, ma'am." He nodded to Aimee and rested his hand on the small of Melah's back and guided her to the passenger door of his vehicle. He opened it and assisted her inside. Once she was secured, he closed the door and walked around the front of the truck.

Aimee still watched him from the stairs. She slowly gave him a nod, then went back inside the building.

He slid into the driver's seat and eyed Melah. The scent of her perfume filled the cab. He didn't know what she wore, but he liked it. It was floral with a hint of warmth and honey.

"I hope Aimee wasn't too hard on you," Melah said.

"Nothing I can't handle." He chuckled. He started the truck and guided them down the main road of the ranch. It was still quite warm outside, and the sun as still shining. They rolled the windows down to allow fresh air to blow inside . "It's nice that you two look out for one another."

"Yeah. It's only the two of us at the moment, so us girls gotta stick together."

"You haven't had any issues with anyone on the ranch, have you?" He stiffened slightly. He quickly glanced over at her. Unprofessional conduct would not be tolerated at the Silver Creek. His father and Buck didn't play those types of games. All were welcomed on the ranch, but if someone treated any of the women inappropriately, it would be dealt with.

"Of course not. Everyone has been cool and welcoming," she said.

"Good. If you do run into any issues, don't hesitate to say something."

Melah nodded at him and turned to stare out of her window.

He switched the radio on, and country music blared out of the speaker. He fumbled to lower the volume. "Shit."

"Someone was jamming." Melah giggled. She tucked her dark thick hair behind her ear.

He rolled his eyes at her. They arrived at the main highway. He brought his truck to a stop before turning onto the road. It wouldn't take long for them to get into town from the ranch.

"Guilty. Some days I like to roll with the windows down with the music on full blast to unwind," he admitted. The last few days had been rough with the on calls blowing up. After he'd dropped the samples off at the clinic, he'd rolled the windows down, cranked the music up, and jammed all the way home.

"Ain't nothing wrong with that. I do my best singing in the car."

"You sing?"

"You know what a screeching banshee sounds like?" Melah arched an eyebrow. Her plump lips were curved up slightly.

The need to find out if they were as soft as they looked weighed heavy on him. He wanted to pull the truck over and bring her into his arms so he could taste them, but Aimee's warning surfaced.

She has nightmares. Bad ones.

What nightmares did she have? What had happened to her? Was that the reason she always appeared guarded? Someone like Melah shouldn't have to suffer alone. She was a good woman with a big heart. He had learned that just by being in her presence for a short while.

"I can't say that I do." He tore his gaze from her and put it back on the road. It wouldn't look good for him if he ran them off the road because he couldn't stop staring at the exquisite woman beside him.

"Well, you would if you listened to me sing."

They shared a laugh. He loved to hear the sound of her laughing and made a note to try his best to do what he needed in order to hear it again.

"So where are we going?" she asked. "I tried to search for the different restaurants in town."

"It's not that many in Ironhaven. If you want more options we'd have to go a town over, but Ironhaven does have some great options. I figured we'd stop at Sunrise Kitchen. They have some really nice food and just opened a few months ago."

"Oh, I didn't see that online." She pulled her cellphone from her purse and swiped at the screen.

"It's new. The owner is the granddaughter of one of my clients. She moved here last year and finally opened her diner."

"Found it. Oh, the menu looks good. I am famished and I'm going to warn you. I like to eat," she said with a wide grin.

She patted her stomach, and Ridge couldn't help but watch her hand. His gaze slid down even farther and stopped at her thick thighs. The fantasy of her soft, bare thighs came to mind. He tore his eyes away and met her gaze.

"Me, too."

Ridge respected any woman who enjoyed food. He glanced across the table at Melah who currently worked on her barbecue ribs dinner. They had arrived at the perfect time. They were able to be seated immediately. Now there was a wait for tables. The decor was modern with a country kitchen flair to it. The color palette of the establishment was whites, tans and browns, and had a homey feel to it.

Frankie had outdone herself with the diner, and so far, the townsfolk of Ironhaven loved it. Her food was rich with flavor, filling, and had one wanting to come back for more. Ridge had eaten here on several occasions and had tried many things so far, but his favorite had to be the short ribs and risotto meal. The meat was so flavorful and melted off the bones. Frankie had a talent that was not going to waste.

"This was a good choice." Melah wiped her hands on her napkins and reached for her drink.

"I'm glad you are enjoying yourself." He sat back and exhaled slowly.

He wanted to enjoy the food and actually taste it and savor it besides just shoveling it in his mouth. The atmosphere was pleasant with soft rock playing from hidden speakers. Servers moved around taking care of the customers. There was plenty of laughter as patrons enjoyed themselves.

"I am. I guess I should have been exploring the town a little more. When I got here, I wanted to dive straight into the ranch and learn my job and stuff. I figured I'd learn about the town later."

"That seems reasonable. How long do you plan to stay on at the ranch?" He reached for his Coke and took a sip. The length of time hands stayed was up to them. They'd had people for a couple months to those who'd stayed on permanently.

"Not quite sure. I wanted to see how everything would be at first, but now that I've met everyone and I actually do like it, I was thinking at least six months." She took her fork and stabbed a large piece of her broccoli. She took a bite out of it and moaned slightly. "Even the vegetables are so damn good."

"Yeah, they are." The sound of her moan went straight to his cock. He watched her tongue sneak out and slide along her bottom lip. The air in his lungs burned, reminding him to inhale. He coughed slightly and took another sip of his Coke.

He couldn't sit here and fantasize about Melah naked, spread out on his bed. No, that wasn't right.

"All this food, I'm going to have to go for a run in the morning." She laughed, reached for her large cornbread muffin, and tore it in half. She took another bite—another moan escaped her. "Damn, this is so good and buttery, too."

Ridge shifted in his seat. His cock had a mind of its own and pushed against his jeans. He had to think of other things. Her moans were driving him crazy. It wasn't the sound of them, it was the fact he wanted to hear them louder and her saying his name while he pushed inside her.

He tore his gaze from her and caught sight of Frankie, the owner, walking around greeting customers. Her eyes met his, and he gave her a little wave to come over to their table. Her smile widened, and she made her way over.

"Hey, Ridge. How the hell are you?" Frankie's warm golden skin practically glowed. Her hair was pulled up in a high ponytail.

He pushed back from the table, stood, and gave her a short hug. "I'm good. How's your grandfather doing? I haven't been out to his farm in a while."

"That old fart is doing just fine." She laughed,

turned to Melah, and offered her hand. "Hi, I'm Frankie. I own this place."

"Hello. I'm Melah. It's so nice to meet you. I'm in love with you—I mean your food." Melah took Frankie's hand.

She moved to stand, but Frankie motioned for her to remain seated. Ridge sat back down.

"Please don't get up. I'm happy you are enjoying the food." Frankie pointed at Ridge. "This one is here at least once a week. He's helping keep me in business."

"Nothing like supporting a small business," he teased.

"Well, I see why Ridge is here so often. I'm new to town, and this is the first restaurant I've tried," Melah admitted.

"You will find Ironhaven does have its gems. Like me, we all use nearby farms for almost everything. I love supporting the local economy." Frankie had been determined to utilize all the farmers around here for all of her meats, dairy, and vegetable needs. She was a respected businesswoman who had cut deals with the residents. That was why so many people loved coming to her diner. Not only was the food cooked to perfection, but the fact everything was locally grown held the interest of the community.

"You want to sit for a minute?" Ridge motioned to the empty chair at their table. He was sure the woman had been working all day. She was a workaholic, and it showed with how well her place was doing.

"If I sit now, I will never get up, but thank you." She smiled and turned her head in the direction of her name being called. "I have to go. It was so nice to meet you, Melah. Please come back soon, and Ridge, I'll see you next week?"

"Of course." Ridge chuckled.

She gave them a wave before dashing over to another table.

"She's so nice." Melah returned to her plate. She picked up her rib and bit off a chunk of meat.

Ridge zoomed in on the sauce that was smeared on the corner of her mouth and her cheek. Without thinking, he scooped up a clean napkin from the table and reached over to blot at the corner of her mouth. She froze in place, her wide brown eyes on him while he wiped the barbecue sauce from her face.

"There. You had a little something on your face." He settled back. He had needed to touch her in some way. Sitting across from the table appeared to be too far.

"Thank you. I appreciate it," she said softly.

"Not a problem." He decided to go back to his food before he did something else crazy. He picked up his fork and snagged a piece of meat and raised it. "So tell me something about you. Where are you from?" He popped the meat in his mouth. It was soft and had been slow cooked for hours.

"Missouri. A little town called Dunwich. It's about an hour and a half west of Jefferson City," she said.

"Your family still there?" Ridge was curious about this woman in front of him. He had the sudden urge to want to discover all there was to Melah.

"Yeah. I'm an only kid. It's just been me and my dad. We moved around a lot because he was in the Army. When he retired, he bought a house around the corner from his brother so we could be close to his family." She flicked her gaze to him, tilted her head to the side, and studied him. "What about you? I already met your brother, Draven. Any other siblings?"

"Nah, my parents could only handle the two of us. My dad said that when I turned two, they realized they were done." Ridge chuckled.

His mother had her hands full when Draven and he were younger. They'd got into everything. When she'd died, there was definitely a change in the house. Nothing had been the same. Andy had tried his best to keep things as normal as possible, but there was always something missing.

"You were a little hellion?" She arched one of her perfectly sculpted eyebrows.

Those plump lips of hers curled up in the corners again. He tried to not focus on them but couldn't help it.

"I mean, define hellion. Was I always pulling pranks, sneaking out, having the school call the house—guilty as charged." He grinned. He had to admit he did have wonderful childhood where love was definitely in the air. There wasn't a day that went by that he didn't remember how much his mother loved him and Draven. The world was cruel to take a woman like Flo Harvey from them.

Andy was never a man to shy away from showing his boys affection. Ridge had grown up admiring the old man. His father had worked hard to make the Silver Creek what it was today.

"What about you?" he asked.

"I was a good girl. Never got in trouble." She

made an imaginary cross on her chest and tried to give off an innocent look.

"Sure you were." Ridge snorted.

"I'm serious. I had good grades all through school, and when I graduated, I knew I was going to enter the Army."

They continued a steady conversation while they finished their food. Once they were done, the waitress came over with the check. Automatically Ridge reached for it, but Melah's hand appeared and pushed his away from the tab.

"My treat, remember?" Melah said.

Ridge grinned and raised his hands in the air. He settled back and allowed her to take the bill.

"I told you I'm not used to this," he said.

She pulled her card from her wallet and waved down the waitress who hadn't waited for payment. The woman returned and took Melah's card and the bill.

"I'll be right back," the waitress said. She spun on her heel and walked away.

Melah turned her attention back to him with a silly grin. "You mean to tell me that there's not one woman who has scooped you up and treated you to dinner?"

"You are the first." His smile slowly faded. At the

moment, he didn't want to think of any other woman. He had a beautiful one in front of him who he wanted to get to know better. There was an attraction between them, and he was sure she felt it, too.

"Why aren't you taken? Why isn't there a Mrs. Ridge Harvey?" Her smile slowly disappeared.

The waitress returned at that moment, giving Ridge time to think of the answer. Why wasn't he married? He couldn't say there hadn't been candidates. He'd dated plenty, had a few steady girlfriends with Raquel being the last serious relationship.

Melah signed her copy of the bill and handed it to the waitress.

"Thanks for stopping by. Enjoy the rest of your night," the waitress said, leaving their table again.

Melah placed her card back inside her purse, turning back to him.

"So...why is there no Mrs. Harvey?" Melah asked again.

Ridge ran a hand along his jawline and didn't have any other answer but the truth.

"Just haven't met the right one yet." He jerked his chin to her. "How about you? Why isn't there a mister out there somewhere?"

"There almost was, but then he showed me who

he truly was." She reached for her drink and finished it off.

He was now even more curious about the woman. What man would fumble her? Whoever he was, Ridge would have to one day thank him.

He blinked. Did he want to pursue her? He took one look at her again and knew without question that he wanted her.

"Have any room left?" He wasn't ready for the night to be over.

Her face relaxed again, and her small smile returned. "What do you have in mind?"

"Ice cream. There's a place not too far from here that has the best ice cream, and this would be my treat," he said.

"Lead the way, Doc."

Chapter Seven

"I don't think I need to eat for the next three days." Melah groaned, sat back in Ridge's truck, and rubbed her belly.

After dinner, he'd taken her for ice cream and, as promised, it was the best she'd ever had. She'd been brave and asked for two scoops, and their scoops were monstrous. She was even tempted to undo the top button of her jeans but resisted.

"I tried to tell you the scoops were large." He chuckled.

He had warned her, but usually when people said big scoops, they really weren't that big. The amount of ice cream they'd given her should have been a crime.

But she'd eaten it all.

There was no way she was going to let ice cream go to waste. They also had donuts at the shop. She'd grabbed a plain glazed for Daisy. She planned to check on her before she headed in for the night.

"Whatever." She hid her smile.

Ridge had been a gentleman and helped her eat some of her ice cream. Tonight had been wonderful. She couldn't remember the last time she'd enjoyed herself so much. Everyone in town appeared to know Ridge. He'd stopped and chatted with random people, then introduced her to them. Not that she was going to remember any of their names, but everyone knew Dr. Harvey. He'd even encouraged a few of them to call his office for some issues they had with their animals.

"You want me to drop you off at the bunkhouse or do you want to go check in on Daisy?" he asked.

He'd given her a side-eye when she'd purchased the donut, but when she'd explained it was for Daisy, he hadn't said a word. Her horse loved a sweet treat, too, and after not being able to work today, Melah figured she'd treat her girl to a good donut.

"You can take me to the barn. I want to give Daisy her donut. I also need to check in on her foot and dressing."

"I can do that if you want while I'm here," he offered.

"Hmmm...I want to do it, but would you mind watching to make sure I do it right?"

Daisy was her responsibility, and she wanted to make sure she could do it. She couldn't have Ridge changing it all the time. He had plenty else to do on the ranch and with his practice.

"I don't mind overseeing." He pulled onto the dirt road that led to the barn.

They fell into a comfortable silence. It was amazing to her that even though she'd only known Ridge for a short time, she felt completely relaxed around him. That usually did not come right away. After her ordeal with Theo, she'd been leery of new people, but for some strange reason she couldn't explain, Ridge was different.

He drove up to the barn and killed the engine.

"Here we are." He slipped out of the truck and walked around the front of the vehicle.

Melah tracked him with her eyes. The confident way he handled himself had her squeezing her legs together. The man was the epitome of sexiness. He arrived at her door and opened it, then held his hand out for her.

The man was a complete gentleman. Pierce had

stopped opening the door or assisting her in his car about six months into their relationship. After they'd broken up, she'd thought of all the red flags in their relationship. There were so many she'd ignored because she'd tried to give him the benefit of the doubt.

"Thank you." She slid her small hand into his larger one and allowed him to help her down. She tilted forward and lost her balance slightly. Her body fell into his. "Oops. I'm so sorry."

Her body was flush against his as he helped lower her to where her feet rested on the ground. His hand remained on her hip, and he hadn't stepped back from her. She tilted her head back to meet his gaze. The moon was high, set against the perfect nighttime backdrop with a few stars scattered across it. The sounds of the night greeted them. The occasional cow lowed, but otherwise nature's orchestra was in full swing off in the distance.

"I got you." His voice rumbled in his chest.

She inhaled sharply. The scent of his cologne had been teasing her all night. She didn't know what it was, but she wanted to nuzzle her face into the crook of his neck and breathe it in.

"You all right?"

"Yeah. I think my foot got caught on something," she whispered. She couldn't look away from his bright-blue eyes. Her hand came to rest on his chest above his heart. The gentle beat thudded against her palm. Melah's moved it up his hardened chest. She didn't know what was coming over her, but she wasn't going to stop now.

She cupped his cheeks. He didn't shy away from her. She studied his face as if to memorize every inch of it. He leaned into her touch. She stood on her tiptoes while he stared down. She guided his face to hers. She touched her lips to his in a soft kiss. She groaned the moment her mouth opened for him. She may have initiated the kiss, but Ridge took over. He gripped her to him, holding her firmly while the kiss deepened.

Melah held on to him as if her life depended on it. She hadn't been kissed like this in so long. Ridge's tongue boldly thrust forward and swept inside her mouth. She closed her eyes and relished the moment of being in his arms. The warmth of his body, the hard planes, and the bulge pressing into her stomach had her whimpering.

He moved them to where her back was flush to his truck. She didn't care at the moment. This had her feeling desired, wanted, and needed. She was tempted to rip her clothes off and climb this man so he could take her. Her heart slammed against her chest as a groan was ripped from him.

Ridge tore his mouth from hers. The only sounds that greeted her was their panting. The kiss had affected both of them. Ridge rested his forehead on hers.

"Melah. I'm—"

"Don't apologize. Please don't." She opened her eyes and met his gaze. She was the instigator of the kiss. She had been wanting it from the moment she'd met him and she refused to have it ruined because of an apology. He hadn't done anything wrong. "I wanted to kiss you. I've been thinking about it for a while now."

His eyes darkened, and he brushed his thumb along her bottom lip. Her mouth still tingled from their kiss. Her body ached in places that hadn't been awakened by a man in a long while.

"I've been wanting to kiss you, too." His voice was low and sent a wave of desire through her.

"Is that so?" Her heart skipped a beat. When one accused their superior of sexual assault, everything private was brought to light in a trial. She'd had all of the intimate details of her life brought to the forefront. Even though she was not the one on trial, everything about her had been put on display. Her sexual encounters to her job performance.

As if she had welcomed the assault.

Afterwards, she had gone into a dark place. Terri, Issac, and Cora had stood by her side through it all. It was because of them that she was able to even smile. They refused to allow her to fall into a dark depression that she may not recover from. They'd ensured she'd enrolled in therapy. They'd taken care of her and ensured she'd got dressed daily.

Those were her real friends, and she missed them fiercely.

Now, here with Ridge, and his one look had her feeling like a woman. Someone who was desirable. Someone he wanted. The heat in his eyes stole her breath. She hadn't even thought of being with a man until she'd met him.

"Well, if you want to do it again, you can," she whispered playfully.

His lips curled up in the corners with a smirk.

"Is that so?" He lowered his head again, and this time, he pressed a soft kiss to her lips. He lifted his head and stared down into her eyes.

Melah would swear he could see into her soul.

This man was dangerous.

She wasn't here for relationships. She was here as part of a plan to find herself and to figure out what the hell she was going to do in life.

She'd be gone in about six months.

Finding a man hadn't even crossed her mind.

"I better go and check in on Daisy," she whispered. She hated to move. The feeling of him next to her was divine, but she had her horse who needed her. What kind of mom would she be if she didn't go and give Daisy her treat and change her dressing?

"Let's go see about Daisy." He stepped back from her and snagged her purse and the bag with the donut in it. He handed them to her before shutting the door to the truck.

He held out his hand to her. She glanced down at it, and the butterflies in her stomach kicked in. She took his hand and allowed him to lead the way into the barn. A few curious horses peeked their heads out of their stalls at the sounds of their footsteps. They arrived at Daisy's and found her sitting on the floor.

"Hey there, Daisy," Melah called out in a sing-song voice.

Daisy turned her head to them. Her dressing was barely hanging on to her leg. She stood and walked over to them. Her limp wasn't as pronounced, which made Melah feel better.

Melah reached up and rubbed Daisy's head. "Are you feeling better?"

Daisy blew out a deep breath and tried to go after the bag in Melah's hand.

"Smart horse. She knows you brought her something." Ridge chuckled.

"Spoiled horse." In all honesty, she was happy to see that Daisy was acting like herself. The items that Ridge had left were tucked away in the bag that Melah had hanging outside her stall. She hung her purse up on an empty hook and grabbed the bag. She tapped Daisy on the nose. "Move back, girl. We are coming in."

Ridge opened the door and ushered her in. It was evident that he went into doctor mode the second they were standing next to Daisy with the way his gaze swept over the horse.

"Did you miss me?" Melah reached inside the bag and brought out the donut.

Daisy neighed softly. Melah giggled at the way Daisy was careful to take the donut into her mouth. She was such a precious horse. She deserved all of the sweet treats—within reason.

Melah rubbed her hands on the back of her jeans

and blew out a nervous breath. She'd never had to do a wound dressing on a horse before, but she was anxious to try it. At least Ridge was there to guide her.

"You sure you don't want me to do it?" Ridge stood next to Daisy. He slowly stroked the horse's neck.

Daisy, the little hussy, was loving the attention. She blew out a shaky breath and leaned into Ridge.

"Nope. She's my responsibility, and I need to take care of her." Melah bent down and removed the barely hanging on material that was on Daisy's leg.

Her horse automatically lifted it for Melah. With Ridge patiently guiding her, she was able to ensure Daisy's wound was still clean and redressed it. Daisy was the best horse a girl could ask for and had held still while Melah worked.

"I should have brought you two donuts!" Melah stood and rubbed Daisy's nose.

Daisy shook her head and gave her a little sassy neigh in response. Ridge and Melah shared a laugh at the horse who took a few steps away as if to test out the dressing on her hoof.

"Yeah, she will be just fine. You did well in catching the issue early." Ridge stood back and folded his arms.

Melah tried to not grin too wide as she gathered the supplies and tossed them back in the bag.

"Well, I had this amazing doctor stop in to check on her. He apparently knows a little something about horses," Melah teased.

Ridge snorted and opened the door to the stall. They stepped outside of it and shut the door. Melah hung the bag back up on the hook and paused in front of Daisy's stall one last time. Her heart was so full of love for her horse. She couldn't wait to get her back out on the ranch.

"How much longer should I keep her from working?"

"Give her another day or two. I'll look at it to make sure it's healed. I didn't have to cut her too deep, so it should be fine."

Melah nodded and stepped back, satisfied with his response. Daisy loved being out in the open and working. She made Melah's job so much easier. She was an experienced ranch horse who enjoyed working.

"Good." Melah grabbed her purse and swung it up on her shoulder.

They walked in silence through the barn. They arrived outside with Melah stopping to turn to Ridge. She didn't know what to say at this point. It had been so long since she'd kissed a man, much less got involved with one.

"Thanks for letting me treat you for dinner."

"It was my pleasure." His eyes crinkled in the corner as he smiled.

She realized he did that often and that was probably one of the reasons why she was immediately comfortable with him.

"Let me drop you off at the bunkhouse."

"You don't have to, I can—"

"I want to."

Melah paused and looked at him. His smile slowly disappeared. He reached for her hand and took it in his. The warmth covered hers. It was callused from hard work, and the sensation of his hand holding hers had her brain going somewhere carnal. Her breath caught in her throat at the fantasy of his rough palms sliding along her smooth thighs to push them open.

She blinked to erase that image from her mind. Her heart rate had skyrocketed at the thought.

"Okay." In all honesty, she didn't want the night to end. This was one night where she felt whole, like a normal person. Even though it hadn't been considered a date, it had all the feelings of one.

Ridge gave a short nod and guided her back to

his truck. He helped her inside again. She pushed down the giddiness that filled her. The woman inside her liked the feeling he gave her, while a voice of reason tried to kill her high by suggesting he was probably helping her inside again since it was a high truck and she'd almost fallen out of it before.

The ride took a couple of minutes. He parked in the exact spot he had when he'd picked her up. She turned to him and met his gaze. They didn't say anything for a moment, then a bubble of laughter came forth. She didn't know where it was coming from or why.

"What's so funny?" Ridge asked with a smile lingering on his lips. He combed his fingers through his hair and focused on her.

"I don't know." She shrugged. She glanced at the house. A soft light glowed in the room where Aimee was staying. She already knew Aimee would wait up until she returned home. If the shoe was on the other foot, Melah would stay up until Aimee made it home safe. "I hadn't figured I would meet someone like you here."

"What is that supposed to mean?" he asked.

"Well, I figured all of the men on the ranch would be older, other soldiers who were like me. You know, fucked up in some kind of way." She truly hadn't known what to expect. She'd been so focused on the fact the ranch offered a way for a person to get on their feet that she hadn't thought she'd meet someone as handsome and kind as Ridge.

Someone she was wanting to have a physical relationship with. Her legs clamped together with that thought.

"Well, you aren't too far off the mark. Most of the hands are ugly sons of bitches."

That brought a giggle out of her.

He reached over and held her hand. "And just because I smile and joke, don't mean that something's not off up here." He pointed to his head. He lifted her hand to his mouth and pressed a soft kiss to the back of it.

She tilted her head and regarded him again. Did Ridge have skeletons in his closet? He had served, too, so there was quite a possibility. He hid it well if he did.

"You better head in. Aimee has peered out the window at least twice since I've parked."

Melah looked over at the house and, sure enough, Aimee was watching them from the window. He was right. She'd better go in before Aimee came out to check on them.

"I really enjoyed myself tonight," she said.

He released her hand, and she felt saddened by it. She liked the feeling of his larger one holding hers. She gripped her purse to keep from reaching for him again.

"I did, too. We should do it again, but maybe next time I'll do the paying."

"What? You didn't like having a woman pay for your meal?" she teased.

Not Ridge, being chauvinistic. He grinned and reached for the handle of his door.

"It's not that I didn't like it, I just prefer to be the one providing a good meal for a beautiful woman." He got out of the truck and shut the door.

Her mouth opened slightly.

He thought her beautiful.

Her cheeks warmed. Was this embarrassment? She'd never done well with compliments. He arrived at her door and opened it.

"Thank you." It was the least she could say. Vernon Battle had taught her manners.

"Now let me help you down so you don't fall again." He held his hand out to her, and this time when she moved to get out, his other hand came to her waist.

She hopped down from the truck.

"See, I can do it. I said something caught on my foot," she muttered.

"Sure, but if it would have happened twice, then I would have known it was done on purpose and I can't help but admit that I liked it." He tossed her a wink. He stepped back from her and shut her door.

Aimee peeked from behind the curtain again. Melah held back a smile at the impatience the woman was exhibiting.

"Whatever." Melah rolled her eyes. She moved her purse strap to her shoulder and motioned to the house. "I better go. Thanks again."

"My pleasure. Have a good night." He gave her a nod and folded his arms.

She waved and walked toward the front door. She didn't need to turn around and see he was watching her. She could practically feel the caress of his gaze on her. A shiver rippled through her.

Melah put a little more sway into her hips as she walked. She arrived at the door and slid her key into it. She opened the door and stepped inside. She turned and found him standing by the driver's door. He saluted and got inside the vehicle. She closed the door and breathed a sigh.

"Have fun?" Aimee came out of the sitting area where she must have been waiting for her. There was a curious look in her eyes, but she didn't say anything else.

At the moment, Melah had to process everything that had happened.

"Yeah, I did." Melah hid the smile that threatened to erupt on her lips. She kicked off her shoes and scooped them up. "I'm off to bed. Work will be here before I know it."

Chapter Eight

"Hey, Doc, would you mind taking a peek at this X-ray?" Heath asked from Ridge's office door. The experienced vet tech had been with Ridge for a few years now, and if he was asking for Ridge to look at something right away, that didn't sound good.

Ridge had only just sat down after seeing countless patients in the office. He and Faith had been extremely busy with a flood of appointments. From dog attacks to an emergency C-section of a goat that had been brought in, to sick guinea pigs to a wellness check for a goose. It had been one hell of a day.

"Sure thing." Ridge pushed up from his chair and followed Heath through the halls of the clinic toward the radiology area. He had just heated up his coffee for the third time, and it looked as if it was going to go cold again. Maybe it just wasn't meant for him to drink his much-needed caffeine source. "What do we have?"

"A golden was brought in. The parents said he hadn't been eating and they thought he was in pain. Dr. Giles was to see him, but she got pulled into an emergency surgery. I went ahead and did the X-ray, but I needed someone to look at it." Heath gave a few more details of the case as they arrived at the reading room.

The film was already up for Ridge to review, and he immediately saw the issue.

"Hmm..." He folded his arms and took another second to make sure he wasn't missing anything else, but he already knew the problem. "How old is the dog?"

"A little over a year," Heath answered.

"Well, it would look like our patient has been a bad boy. He's eaten something he shouldn't have." Ridge pointed to the foreign object that shouldn't be inside the retriever. The dog's stomach had tried to pass it along, but it was now stuck in the intestines, and that was why the animal wasn't eating and the parents were correct. He was probably in a world of pain. Looked like Ridge was about to scrub in for surgery. "Where are they? I'll go speak with them now."

"Thanks. They are in room four. Want me to get the other OR suite ready?" Heath would be assisting on the case.

"Please." Ridge slapped Heath on the shoulder and walked through the busy clinic. He arrived at the golden's room and pushed open the door. "Hey there, family."

He introduced himself and could see the worry on the couple's face. The dog was lying on the floor, panting in obvious pain. He went over the X-ray with the parents.

"When can the surgery be done? Our kids will go insane if something happen to Jimbo." The woman sniffed. She reached up and wiped a lone tear from her eye.

"I have time now. This would be considered an emergency. With the object being positioned in the bowel, Jimbo won't be able to pass this. Not taking this out will lead to extreme pain, sepsis, and eventually death." Ridge had to be careful when speaking with families about their beloved animals, but he was going to be honest. Animals were brought in all of the time having eaten something they shouldn't. "This would be standard surgery, and with Jimbo being young, I don't foresee any possible complications, but they can happen. Jimbo will be running around and eating again within a few days."

"Okay, please. Do whatever you have to do to save our pup. He's like our third child," the man said.

"Doc, we trust you. Please take care of our baby." The woman reached down and gave Jimbo a pat on his head.

Ridge offered a small smile at the dog's tail waving slightly. That was a good sign.

"We certainly will. Just give us a few minutes, and Heath will be back here to get Jimbo."

Ridge shook both of their hands then left. He shut the door and made his way back toward the surgical suites. He paused at his phone buzzing in his pocket. He pulled it out and read a message from his father asking for him to come check in on a new calf that was born today with a deformed snout. He quickly responded and continued on. After his surgery, he could head out to the ranch.

It had been two days since his dinner with Melah, and she hadn't been far from his mind. The kiss they'd shared had done something to him. Her soft lips and the sound of her moan when he'd backed her up against the truck had replayed in his mind repeatedly.

Well, if you want to do it again, you can.

Her words echoed in his head. He wanted to do more than kiss her. What he wanted may even scare her. He could see the slight hesitation in her. He wasn't sure what had happened to her, but he'd have to be careful, let her set her own pace with them.

And there would be a 'them'.

Her desire for him was evident. She felt the connection between them. There was no doubt with the way she'd initiated their first kiss.

Ridge entered the suite. Heath had everything set up for him. Unfortunately for Jimbo, there would be no endoscopy procedure to extract whatever it was he'd eaten. That would have been ideal if the object had remained in his stomach. Ridge was going to have to open him up to get the object out.

"I'm going to go ahead and bring Jimbo back," Heath said.

Ridge figured he'd do a little work while Heath grabbed Jimbo. He quickly logged in and answered a few emails. Pretty soon, Heath had Jimbo in the room and up on the surgical table. The poor pup whimpered, and Ridge's heart went out to him. This was what he had always dreamed of when he was a kid. Helping sick animals had always been close to his heart. He moved over to the table to help Heath get an IV line placed so they could administer fluids and the medication that would sedate the animal while Ridge worked.

Once the pup was asleep, they quickly began. Surgery didn't take long, and Ridge had to chuckle when he pulled the foreign object out of the pup's intestines.

"Well, Jimbo, your mother is going to be shocked when she sees what you ate."

Jimbo had consumed a woman's small underwear—a thong to be exact.

"Oh my." Heath laughed.

He shook his head and offered a sterile silver bowl for Ridge to drop the underwear in. They'd bag it up and give it to the family later if they wanted it. Some families liked to keep the items removed from their pets as keepsakes, and Ridge was sure they also used them for conversation starters.

"Can't say we haven't seen this before. I just hope it's the mom's and not anyone else's."

Ridge drove on the Silver Creek Ranch and inhaled sharply. The fresh air flowing through the open windows gave him his second wind. Fatigue had set in, but he was going to have to ignore it for now. After discussing the outcome of Jimbo's surgery with the parents, he'd had to see two more patients before he'd been able to leave to go out to the ranch.

He called his father to find out where the new calf was located so he could go check him out.

"Hey, Ridge. Are you on the ranch?" Andy's gravelly voice came onto the line.

"Yeah. I just got here. Where is the calf?" Ridge ran a hand along his face and grimaced from the amount of stubble that greeted him. At the rate he was going, he should let it keep growing and see what he looked like with a beard.

"He's out in the southern pasture. Melah is with him. The momma rejected him and tried to hurt him," Andy said.

Ridge sighed. It was always a trying case when the new mommas rejected their babies. It could be because of the deformity or just the momma didn't bond with the calf when it was born.

"I'm on my way." Ridge disconnected the call and increased his speed. He wasn't sure if it was to get to the animal or to see Melah. Just the thought of being near her again sent his heart racing. His grip tightened on the steering wheel as he guided the vehicle in the direction of the pasture Melah and the calf were.

He slowed down a bit and drove along the dirt road, trying to catch sight of Melah. He finally spotted her sitting on the ground with a black form in front of her. He killed the engine and got out. He went around to the back where his bag was and snagged it. He wasn't sure what to expect but wanted to take his travel supplies with him. There were plenty of times he'd had to do impromptu procedures on the ranch.

He stalked toward Melah, and his heart stuttered. She reached up and wiped her face with the back of her arm.

Was she crying?

Had the calf died?

He picked up speed.

She turned and glanced over her shoulder. A small smile came to her lips. "Hey there, Doc."

"Is everything okay?" Ridge immediately dropped next to her and placed his bag down. The physician in him assessed the calf the moment he laid eyes on him. Its body looked normal. Sizing was good. He appeared healthy except for his face. His snout was tilted to the side, and there was a gap between his lip and the inside of his mouth.

"Yeah. I just got really emotional watching the mom kick and push him away. She wouldn't allow him to nurse." Another tear slid down her face as she rubbed her hand along the calf's neck. She lifted the half-empty bottle. "I figured I'd try to get him to eat something."

"Did he drink any?" Ridge reached for the calf. The small black cow tried to pull away, but Ridge kept a firm grip on him. He did a quick peek at his eyes and opened his mouth so he could check inside. It didn't seem as if there were any other issues with the calf besides the gap and the twisted snout.

"A bit. He seemed to get tired, so I was giving him a break," Melah said.

He reached for his bag and removed his stethoscope. Her quiet gaze caused the hairs on the back of his neck to rise. He listened to the calf's chest and stomach, and everything appeared to be normal. He dropped the stethoscope on the ground and tried to urge the calf up on its feet.

"Is he okay?" Melah asked.

"He should be."

The calf stood on his weak and wobbly legs. It glanced around, and its gaze landed on Melah. It took a few steps toward her. She stood and met it. Its gaze was on the bottle.

"Go ahead. See if he will take the bottle. I want to see how well he sucks on the nipple."

Melah gave a nod and offered the bottle. The calf took to the bottle and began drinking. A small amount of milk came out. It wasn't going to be as bad as he'd thought. The little guy would be different than the others but should be fine.

Melah sniffed again and let out a curse. She wiped her face with her shoulder.

"He's going to be okay." Ridge rested a hand on her shoulder.

She looked at him with her two big brown eyes filled with tears.

He nodded to the calf who had almost finished the bottle. "It happens quite often. Heifers reject their babies, and we take over and become their parents. He'll grow to be strong and a regular bull or steer. We'll just have to keep an eye on him to ensure he's eating well."

"That's good to hear." She tugged the empty bottle away from the calf and rubbed his head.

He stumbled away from her and gazed around at the open grassy area. She sniffed again, and Ridge felt her emotions were about more than the calf being rejected from his mother.

"What's really going on, Melah?" He moved next to her and took her free hand in his.

Her gaze flicked to his for a brief moment before she turned away. A shaky chuckle escaped her.

"It's just that, I know how the calf feels," she whispered. She used the back of her arm to wipe her face again.

He drew her to him.

"What do you mean?" he asked quietly.

"My mom didn't want me either. She gave up her rights to me the moment I was born." She wouldn't meet his gaze.

He used a finger to tip her chin up so she'd look at him.

She sniffed again. "My dad knew he wanted me from the moment he'd found out she was pregnant. She signed away her rights and left the hospital the day after I was born. My father said he hasn't seen her since that day."

Ridge studied the strong woman in front of him. She had done extremely well for herself. She had survived being a woman enlisted in the Army. She was a hard worker on the ranch. She had much to be proud of. He may not know her full story, but from what he did know, he was impressed by her.

He couldn't even begin to know how it would feel to know that his mother didn't want him. His had been loving, kind, and nurturing. It was a damn shame she was taken too soon from them, but at least he had gotten to know her and felt her love for him

"Oh, Melah," he exhaled. He brought her flush to him and wrapped an arm around her shoulders.

She leaned into him, pressing her face to his chest. Her shoulders shook while no sounds escaped her.

"I'm so sorry," he said.

"It's nothing you need to be sorry for. I'm sorry I got so emotional. Who would have thought seeing a baby calf get rejected by his mother would have me acting like this." She barked a shaky laugh. She reached up and wiped at the trail of tears.

His hand found its way to her face. He used his thumb to wipe away the wetness she'd missed.

"There's nothing wrong with showing emotions. Animals are always a weak spot for me," he admitted.

"I doubt someone like you cries over an abandoned cow." She snorted.

"Maybe not an abandoned cow since I've been around them practically my whole life, but when I have to share with a family that their dog has terminal cancer and won't make it, or the beloved horse has to be put down because of an incurable disease, it's never easy." He stared down into her wide eyes.

She shook her head and lifted her hand to his chest. "I'm glad I don't have your job. That must be rough."

"It can be, but then I think of all of the families I've been able to help, or the smiles on kids' faces when I tell them their animals booboos are going to be okay, or how their pet chicken is just constipated," he said.

That brought a smile to her face. She played with the buttons on his shirt and blew out a shaky breath.

"Thanks." She glanced over at the baby cow who was swaying on his weak legs. Later today he should be walking around more confident. "So what do we do about him?"

"Well, he's going to have to be bottle fed until he's weaned and then he can join the herd. We can try to see if another momma will be willing to adopt him," he said.

"Can I choose a name for him?" Melah's eyes widened as if she'd need to bribe him. She could name any of the cows if she wanted to. Most of them were just identified by their tag numbers.

"Sure. What do you have in mind?" He rested his arm on her shoulders and pulled her into him as the calf wobbled around.

"Reggie. I think he looks like a Reggie," she said with a nod.

Ridge couldn't hold back the laugh that erupted from him. "Reggie?"

"Yeah, Reggie. I don't want to call him Reject, but Reggie is close enough. He's going to grow up to be big and strong, and all of the lady cows will be after him." The sadness was gone from her eyes. She gave him a genuine smile and turned to him.

Ridge lifted a hand and cupped her face.

"You are exquisite, Melah." He didn't know what it was about this woman, but her big heart and the way she was able to overcome a painful start in life drew him to her. Melah's lips called to him. He lowered his head and captured them with his. The bottle in her hand fell to the ground, forgotten.

She turned to him and closed the small gap between them.

His lips moved over hers in the most sensual dance. She opened herself to him. His tongue slipped inside her mouth and caressed hers. He didn't want to rush anything between them. When they made love for the first time—and they would—he was going to ensure they took their time exploring each other.

Ridge grunted at the feeling of Melah pressing closer to him. Her full breasts resting against him had his cock hard as a rock. He slid his hand down her body and cupped her ample ass to hold her in place.

The kiss deepened. He tilted his head, needing to consume her. Something bumped into his leg. He broke the kiss and looked down to find Reggie standing next to them. Melah giggled and reached down to scratch the calf on the head between his eyes.

"Is this bad man keeping my attention from you?" Her giggle floated through the air.

Ridge didn't want to release her from his hold. She turned her attention back to him, and his eyes were drawn to her swollen lips.

"He's had more of your time than me. I just got here," Ridge grumbled. He cupped her face with both hands and pressed another kiss to her lips. He lifted his head slowly and stared into her eyes. "Why don't you come to my place for dinner. We can grill out, there's a pond in the back you can swim in..."

He left his offer open for her. She bit her lip,

tempting him to want to kiss her again. The wheels in her brain were turning. He wasn't sure if she was going to take him up on his offer. They didn't have to do anything. It could just be them spending time getting to know one another.

"Would I need to bring anything?" she asked.

"Just you and maybe a bathing suit," he replied.

She blinked a few times before she nodded. "Okay. That sounds like fun."

Chapter Nine

Melah didn't know why she was so nervous. It wasn't like she was a virgin or anything. She'd had consensual sex before. Even enjoyed it. But something about being at Ridge's house was different. Was she expecting to have sex with Ridge tonight—no.

But it wasn't off the table. If her opportunity came, she was going to take it.

She'd arrived, and he'd showed her around his home which was magnificent. It was tucked away on the ranch surrounded by lush and majestic trees on either side with the lake at the back. She was impressed with the beauty of Silver Creek Ranch.

The property looked as if it could be featured on one of those home and garden television shows. With its weathered stone and wood in the design, it appeared as if they'd used the very trees that were rooted in the area to build it. It had given her the sense of home the moment she'd stepped foot through the front door.

She glanced at herself in the mirror in the bathroom. The only bathing suit she'd brought with her was a two-piece she'd picked up on the spur of the moment before coming to Ironhaven. It was bright pink and orange and showed off her ample curves. It looked really good on her, and now that she was seeing herself in it again, she remembered why she'd picked it up.

She was sexy as hell in it.

"You can't hide in here forever." She snagged her bag and draped it over her shoulder. She navigated through the house until she came to the kitchen. Her breath was immediately snatched from her as she saw the view. The floor plan was open with the kitchen flowing into an eating area and then the living room. Windows stretched from wall to wall, showcasing the alluring, vibrant South Dakota landscape that included the crystal-clear lake the house was built along.

The scent of hickory and wood filled her nostrils. She inhaled sharply, and her stomach growled.

"Something smells good." Melah stepped out onto the wide cedar deck that stretched out over the water and shut the door behind her.

The late afternoon sun basked them in warmth. Ridge was dressed in swim trunks and a t-shirt. He shut the lid to the grill and turned to her. He paused, his heated gaze raking over her.

Something inside her clicked.

She liked the way he looked at her. She held her head high and walked over to one of the multiple cushioned loungers and dropped her bag down. Her skin prickled from Ridge's stare. He'd set towels out for them to use for the pond. He hadn't been playing when he'd said there was a pond in his yard.

She admired the scenery, captivated by the emerald shoreline on the other side of the water. A few birds flew overhead while the water rippled slightly. A gentle breeze blew, carrying the scent of pine and summer. Ridge's place gave the sense of healing, and it was no wonder the man was able to smile so often.

"Ready for a dip?" Ridge's voice came behind her.

She turned and found him standing without his shirt, a towel perched on his shoulder and one in his hand. Her mouth went dry as she caught sight of the fine planes of his muscular physique. She swallowed hard, her gaze sliding down to his abdomen that had distinguished lines and a sprinkle of hair that disappeared underneath his shorts.

She tore her gaze from him and cleared her throat. Her core pulsed with the thought of what waited for her beneath those shorts.

"Yeah."

He grasped her hand in his and led her to the stairs that took them directly down into the water. It had been a while since she'd swum, and she looked forward to it. She'd learned at an early age, thanks to her father. With the hard work she'd been doing on the ranch, a swim was just what she needed to relax her muscles.

"We can hang the towels here. I put these hooks—"

"Oh, what about the food?" Melah glanced back over at the large black grill with smoke coming from under the lid. What if the food burned? As hungry as she was, she honestly wouldn't care about eating burned food. It wouldn't be the worst thing she'd eaten.

"I just lit it. I want the coals to settle down. We can go for a swim first, then I'll throw the steaks on." Ridge smiled and brought her flush to him. He must have seen the longing in her eyes. He pressed a kiss to her forehead then tipped her chin up to meet her eyes. "Don't worry. I'm going to take care of you."

"You better," she teased.

A small smile appeared on her lips. His eyes darkened with something she couldn't read, and her stomach quivered with anticipation. She had a feeling he wasn't speaking of food, and neither was she.

Her heart skipped a beat at his confident smirk. He tossed their towels onto the large hooks on the railing. He turned quickly and lifted her by the back of her knees. She squealed and held on to his broad shoulders as he took a leaping bound and jumped into the air over the water.

"Ridge!" she shouted, but then they hit the water.

Even though it was warm outside, the water had a nice chill to it at first. She moved her arms through the water as she broke the surface. She turned and found him laughing. "Hey, you could have at least warned me."

She couldn't help the smile that formed on her lips. She leaned back and allowed herself to float on her back while gazing at the lovely sky.

"Where's the fun in that?" Ridge snickered.

He dove underneath the water out of sight. Her heart rate skyrocketed as she flipped over and tried to find him. She swam a few strokes away. Where the hell did he go? A hand snaked around her ankle and tugged her underneath.

"Hey!" Melah yelped.

She sank underneath, and arms wrapped around her. There was no sense of fighting him off. If anything, she wanted to move closer to him. She hadn't felt this safe with a man in a long time. Melah didn't know what to think. Instead, she decided to live in the moment. She didn't know what tomorrow would bring, but she was going to accept the inevitable between her and Ridge. They broke the surface with her still in his embrace. Her smile widened at the look on his face. This man was a goofball. How did she get so lucky to meet someone like him?

"Having fun?" she asked.

"I am now." He grinned and brought her closer to him, not leaving any room between them.

Melah leaned into him and wrapped her arms around his neck. She didn't want to leave the warmth of his embrace. A shiver rippled through her at the feel of his naked chest against her. She inhaled and basked in the moment.

A warm, late summer day. A sexy cowboy who had a heart of gold and loved working with animals.

And whose attention was on her.

She tightened her hold on him and didn't break his gaze.

"I love it when you smile," he murmured.

Her breath caught in her throat. Their legs brushed each other as they moved to keep them afloat.

"You've certainly given me something to smile about," she whispered.

Life had been getting her down. She was determined to not let it, and when she was around him, he was a wonderful distraction. She'd thought hard work on a ranch would do it, but funny how it was the devilishly handsome vet who filled her thoughts.

"Good." His head swooped down, and his lips covered hers.

The kiss was the sweetest thing she'd ever experienced. His warm lips coaxed hers open to allow his tongue to sweep inside. She welcomed him, his presence and everything about him. Melah didn't want today to end.

She slid her fingers along the nape of his neck and entwined them in his thick hair. She pressed closer to him, wanting to feel all of him.

And she certainly could feel the large bulge that rested against her belly. She gasped and tore her mouth from his. He may want to see her smile more, but he just didn't know how competitive she was or how she always got her revenge.

She moved back to kiss him again. His eyes closed, and she took her opportunity to use her weight to dunk him underneath the water. A laugh tore from her as his arms flailed out when he went under. She spun around and swam away as fast as she could.

She hadn't felt this free in ages.

"That's what we do?" he hollered behind her.

She glanced over her shoulder. He was cutting through the water at a much faster speed then she'd anticipated.

Shit!

He'd been in the Navy. Of course he moved like a fish in water.

She shrieked and tried to go faster, but she was no match for him. Just as he reached for her, she slipped beneath the water and ducked out of his grasp. She took the chance and swam back toward the house, but her plan didn't go the way she'd imagined it.

Arms wrapped around her and brought her to the surface.

"Hey!" she shouted.

Her laughter bubbled out of her. His chuckles rumbled by her ear. He bent his head and nipped her ear.

"You're going to pay for that," he said.

Melah's core clenched at the deep resonance of his voice. Her back was flush against his chest. His strong arms rested along her waist.

"What are you talking about? That was payback for you throwing me in the water," she said.

They were drifting back to the deck of the house. She looked over her shoulder at the twinkle in his blue eyes.

"I assisted you into the water."

"You tossed me—"

"I was holding you as we went in together."

"Same damn thing. You threw us into the water." She finally was able to turn toward him.

His arms tightened around her and kept her near him. At the moment, she didn't want to be anywhere else. Ridge didn't have to worry about her leaving the security or warmth of his embrace.

"Tomay-to. Tomato." He shrugged. His lips were in his infamous crooked grin.

She wrapped her arms around his neck and tilted her head back to watch him.

"Why me?" she whispered. Doubt always had to ruin shit and creep into the back of her mind. She was a broken soldier trying to find her way in life after retirement. What could a man like Ridge want with her? He was where she wanted to be in life. Living out his dreams, secured plans for the future, and a place to call home.

She, on the other hand, had a *concept* of a plan.

"Why not you? Melah, you are beautiful, head-strong, determined, intelligent. I'm drawn to everything there is about you." He gripped her chin. The smile disappeared from his lips as he studied her.

She swallowed hard. Her heart rate jumped up drastically at that moment.

His thumb ran across her bottom lip. "I want to know everything there is about you. You've said you don't know how much time you have here in Iron-haven, but I'm telling you now that I want all of it. Each minute you are here. However long that may be, I want to spend it with you."

"Ridge..." She was left speechless.

She shook her head, but he pressed a finger to her lips.

"I'm serious. I want you, Melah. However or whatever that means."

"But I'm broken. That's why I'm here at Silver Creek. You may not know what it feels like to feel lost. For so many years the Army dictated where I went, what I did—so much of my life, and now that I'm no longer that person, I'm trying to figure out who Melah Battle is, the civilian." Tears clouded her vision.

Dammit, she was not going to cry. Not now. She had been an emotional mess since arriving at Silver Creek. What was going on?

"I get it and I want to be with you while you figure it out. You never know, maybe Silver Creek is where you're supposed to be."

Somehow, they'd made it to the ladder that led up to the deck. Ridge's blue eyes were wide, and there wasn't a speck of deceit that she could see. Ridge Harvey was a good man. Hell, she knew his father, and Andy was one of the best men she'd ever met, and his son was as well. Even Draven, with his big scary ass, was someone she could depend on. The Harveys were upstanding men who'd give a person the last of what they had.

Melah glanced up at the sky and sighed.

This man before her was already claiming a

small piece of her heart. She hadn't come here looking for love or relations, she had come to find herself.

"I'm not going to promise anything, Ridge." She glanced back at him. There was no question there was something between them. One thing she had promised herself was that she was going to live life to the fullest once she was out of the military.

Ridge gave a slight nod. His large hands were a distraction at the moment, screwing with her thought process. One rested on her waist while the other made its way down to her bottom.

This man was dangerous.

But it wasn't like Melah hadn't been in dangerous situations before. She'd run headfirst into plenty of hostile situations in the Army.

This was no different.

Only this time, her heart was at stake.

Melah leaned forward and pressed her lips to his.

Chapter Ten

Melah's legs were wrapped around his waist. He crawled up the ladder out of the water with her holding on to him. Her lips blazed a trail along his jawline and down to his neck. He released a slight curse and hauled them up the final step to the deck.

He stood still and cupped her cheek to bring her face to his. He took her lips in a soul-snatching kiss. She returned it with the same amount of fire that burned within him. Her ass filled his other hand as he held her propped against him. A moan slipped from her, and the sound alone sent an electric current through him. His cock was hard and pressing on his shorts, demanding release.

He hadn't known he'd be spilling his guts to her

in the water. Something about her expression had him sharing what he'd been holding back. But he'd wanted her to know he was serious about her.

She'd been hurt in the past.

He got that. Anyone could see it a mile away. Melah was a strong woman, and Ridge was telling her the truth. He wanted whatever she was willing to give him.

Her soft mounds squished to his chest were so damn tempting. From the moment he'd seen her in the bathing suit, he'd wanted to tear it off her. It left little to the imagination. Melah's body was flawless. It was the perfect combination of curves and muscles. She was all woman. She took care of herself, and this wasn't anything the military could have done for her.

He walked them over to one of the lounge chairs. He took a seat and helped her straddle him. They separated for the brief moment it took for him to get them situated in the chair.

"Ridge..." She raked her fingers through his wet hair.

A tremor racked him at the feel of her fingers on his scalp. Her gaze landed on him. His breath escaped him as if someone had slammed a two-by-four across his stomach.

"Whatever you want," he murmured.

He brought her back down to him and gently kissed her. He didn't want to scare her. Something in her eyes led him to want to give her the control of what they did today. She lifted slightly, breaking the kiss. Their noses were millimeters from each other.

"Whatever?" Her lips tilted up in the corners.

His heart skipped a beat at the glint in her eyes. His cock grew even stiffer as she slowly shifted her bottom. He bit back a groan at the sensation of the material from his shorts rubbing his hard member.

"Whatever," he echoed. His voice was somewhat hoarse. He cleared his throat. He took one of her hands and brought it up to his mouth. Kissed her palm. He then entwined their fingers together. Her hand was much smaller than his and was completely engulfed.

She closed the gap between them, and this time she kissed him. Her plump lips moved over his in a sensual move. They opened, and her tongue snuck out and slipped into his mouth. He welcomed it and allowed his to duel with hers. He wasn't going to take over.

He wanted her to have full control.

Her fingers tightened in his hair as she deepened the kiss. He ghosted his free hand up the smoothness of her back. Her skin was warm and soft. He trailed it down to her lower back and held on to her. She arched her hips and slid along the length of him. The small bit of clothing between them created friction that had a groan erupting from Ridge. He couldn't hold it back any longer.

This gorgeous woman was driving him crazy, but he loved every moment of it.

She explored him. Her lips traced over his face, down to his neck and to his chest. He rested back and allowed her to take her precious time. He wasn't going to rush any of this. Her hands came to a stop on his chest. She lifted her head, and those brown orbs burned trails over him. She watched her hands move across his skin.

She trailed them down to the center of his abdomen. He held his breath. She sat back, her gaze once again coming to meet his. Her bright-pink and orange bathing suit was the perfect contrast of her tawny skin. She reached behind her and undid the ties of the top.

Ridge's heart stopped; the material fell away, revealing her plump mounds with their dark areolas. Her nipples beaded into little buds that called to him. She tossed the top off onto the ground.

Ridge's hands rested on her waist, and he stared

at the perfection before him. He licked his lips and leaned forward to capture one of her mounds in his mouth. He bathed the bud with his tongue before suckling it.

"Ridge," Melah moaned.

Her fingers returned to his hair and gripped it tight. He brought her closer to him and continued to suckle her. His other hand came to capture the other mound. Her breast was large enough to fill his palm. Her skin was soft, supple, and tasted like sunshine. He released the one from his mouth and moved over to the other. She rocked her hips, dragging her heated core over his shaft.

He couldn't get enough of the woman. He'd take his time and receive anything she offered him. He nipped at her hardened bud, eliciting another moan from her. He loved hearing his name on her tongue. He nipped her again and massaged the other one with his hand. He pinched that nipple which had her crying out.

"Ridge!"

He grinned against her skin. He glanced up at her to find her watching him. He released her from his mouth and dragged his tongue over her areola, outlining it before he trailed his tongue across her sternum to the other one. He captured it again and held her gaze, sucking her nipple into his mouth.

Her hips moved again. He dropped his hand to her ass and guided her along him more. Her mouth opened with a small gasp escaping from her.

"I need these clothes off," she whispered. She reached down for the ties of the lower part of her bathing suit. She untied them and then lifted slightly so she could take it off. She dropped the small item on her top.

The remaining breath in Ridge's lungs escaped him. Her waist was tapered in and flared out with her hips, but it was the tiny center area that caught his attention. Her small patch of hair was neat and hid her most secretive place.

Her fingers dropped to the edge of his shorts.

"These must go." Her gaze didn't waver from his.

"Yes, ma'am."

He reached down to shuck them off while still holding on to her. He didn't want her to move from where she was. He tossed the shorts off to the side and gripped Melah flush to him. She wrapped her arms around him and crushed her mouth to his.

This kiss was different. She took what she wanted, and he allowed her to. His hands roamed her soft skin. She rotated her hips and brought her core down his length. He groaned and slipped a hand between them. He parted her folds and found them slick. He thrust his tongue into her mouth, unable to hold back. She arched her back to him as he drove his finger through her slickness. He connected with her bundle of nerves. He immediately stroked her clit.

"Ridge," she moaned.

"Keep saying my name like that," he rasped.

He nipped her on her chin. He soothed it with his tongue then moved down to the column of her neck. He continued to stroke her most sensitive bud. She rode his finger, her hips undulating against his hand. His cock ached in ways he'd had never known before. He ignored it. Now was about Melah. He wanted her to come apart on him. He licked her soft skin while his finger continued its journey. He didn't want to bring her to climax too soon. He wanted to draw this out between them.

He was also selfish enough to want to feel her climax with him buried inside her.

She gripped his head between her hands and tilted his head back. Her lips plundered his, her tongue slipping into his mouth. Their kisses were growing more frantic, her hips moving faster. The wetness from her cunt bathed his fingers and hand. He welcomed all of it.

He needed to make sure she was ready for the first time he entered her. He didn't want there to be any discomfort for her. As much as he wanted to bury his face between her legs, there was plenty of time for that later.

And there would be a later.

"I need—" her voice ended on a moan.

He drew his finger back to her clit and applied pressure, stroking it.

"What do you need, Melah?"

He couldn't take his eyes off her. She was the most enticing creature he'd ever seen. Her eyes were closed as she rode his hand. Her breasts rose and fell with each breath. They were gorgeous, and he could spend all day suckling them. He leaned forward and nipped one of her buds with his teeth.

"You," she gasped. Her eyes opened and met his. There was a fire in them that burned bright. "I need you. In me."

"Put me where you want me."

He removed his hand and brought it to his lips. Unable to resist, he wanted to get a taste of her. He licked his fingers. The taste of her exploded on his tongue. A growl ripped from him.

Oh, he was going to have his wish.

She was going be spread out somewhere so he could drink directly from the source.

"Oh God." She watched him with wide eyes.

He grinned at her and motioned for her to make the first move.

"You want me? You gotta put me there," he murmured.

This was for her, and what she wanted, she was going to have to take. She reached down and wrapped her hand around him. His smile immediately disappeared. The feel of her clenching him almost had him exploding. Maybe this wasn't such a good idea. He tried to think of anything else but the feel of her guiding him to her most intimate area. She rose and nestled the broad head of his cock to her slick opening. He held her waist and tried to not leave bruises.

She slowly lowered herself down on him.

A groan ripped from him at the feeling of her opening for him. Her tight channel gripped him in a warm hug.

"Fuck," he groaned.

She wiggled herself down to take more of him. Melah was tight, hot, and perfect for him.

"Damn. I don't think you'll fit—"

"I'll fit. Relax," he tried to coax her.

He clamped her hips and lifted her slightly. Her eyes were closed, and he helped guide her down. She bit her bottom lip, sinking farther down on him. Her hands rested on his shoulders. Her nails bit into his skin, but he ignored the slight pain.

He held the base of his cock steady. She maneuvered her way down until she was fully seated on him. They released simultaneous groans. He held her to him. Her warm cocoon was absolute heaven, and he didn't want to ever move. She repositioned herself to where her arms were wrapped around his neck, leaving her breasts crushed between them.

"I'm so full. Ridge, I can't—"

"You can," he bit out. He raised her then brought her back down. Her muscles relaxed around him. "See how you can take me. You fit around me perfect."

Her moan did nothing but make him want her more. He wanted to pound away until he was no more, but he had to remember, this was for her. He brought her face down to him and kissed her lips.

"Take, baby. Take what you need," he encouraged.

Her eyes opened. They were filled with lust and desire. She nodded slightly, her teeth coming out to snag her bottom lip. He wanted to yank her teeth away from it and soothe it with his tongue. She tilted her head back and rode him. He grunted with the sensation of her warm silkiness sliding along his length. He held her, watched her.

Her eyes were closed, and she did as he'd commanded.

Took what she needed.

She was a magnificent sight. Her hips undulated in a sensual rhythm. Ridge leaned forward and captured one of her tempting mounds in his mouth. He had to keep himself busy to try to distract himself from releasing early. He'd be damned if he came first. He teased her nipples with the attention of his mouth and hand.

Her moans grew louder, and he loved the sounds of them mixed in with sighs and his name. Her fingers came to entangle in his hair, which he loved. She surrounded him completely.

This was what he wanted.

What he needed.

It wasn't selfish of him. He took his enjoyment from her pleasure. She rode him with wild abandon. She finally relaxed and let go. Her movements quickened. Her nails dug into his scalp, but he couldn't care less.

"Fuck. Melah. Keep going," he rasped.

He slipped a hand between them and found her swollen bundle of nerves. He gathered her slickness and brought it to her clit and stroked her in quick motions. She cried out, and her muscles spasmed around him.

"That's it, baby. Let go."

Her pleasure took hold of her. Melah's body trembled. He gripped her with one hand while the other remained on her clit. He thrust upward, matching her rhythm. The sounds of their lovemaking filled the air. Her body shook, her climax taking hold of her.

"Ridge!" she screamed.

Her muscles clamped down on him while she rode the waves of her orgasm. A warmth flooded around his cock from her. She wrapped her arms around him, bringing his head to her chest. He withdrew his other hand so he could hold her steady to pound harder into her.

His hips were on autopilot. He couldn't fill her enough. He grunted, and the signs of his own climax rushed toward him. Her warmth covered him, and her muscles squeezed him, and finally, he couldn't hold back any longer.

A roar burst from him; his release shot out of

him. Thick ropes of his seed jetted inside her. Melah's channel milked every ounce from him. His breath was snatched. He closed his eyes and held her. His hips thrust forward one last time, and more of him poured into her. She held on until he finally grew still, his cock still buried inside her.

He couldn't move if he tried. His heart pounded like a horse galloping along the open lands. He pressed small kisses to her neck and her chin. No words were needed. Her body rested on him. Her chest was rising and falling just as fast as his was. They were both rendered breathless with the sounds of their pants mixing with the distant calls of nature in the surrounding woods.

They remained that way for what seemed forever. Her warm cocoon was a place he never wanted to leave. His cock was semisoft, and it wouldn't take much for him to be ready again. That was how much he wanted this woman. A light sheen of sweat covered their bodies. She shifted slightly in his hold and nuzzled his neck with her face.

He left kisses along her shoulder. He glanced over it at the beauty of his property, and it resonated in him—she had to stay.

She may not know it yet, but this was where she belonged. She may need to find herself, but he was as sure as the days were long that this was where she was supposed to be.

On the Silver Creek Ranch and in his arms.

Forever.

Now he was going to have to convince her of this.

She moved her hips, and that was all it took. His cock grew hard again. She lifted her head and stared down at him. Her big brown eyes widened, and a small smile lingered on her lips.

"Already? Really?"

"Really," he murmured.

He brought her down and kissed her softly. She rotated her hips, which drew a moan from him. He broke the kiss and smiled.

"I'm not done with you yet, Melah Battle. We're just getting started. I'm going to show you how much I need you."

Chapter Eleven

Melah couldn't erase the silly grin from her lips. Warm arms wrapped around her from behind. She tried to pull away from them, but their owner was stronger than her. Ridge's warm chest pressed on her back. The man was insatiable. He hadn't been lying when he'd said he'd show her how much he needed her. She cleared her throat and again tried to stop grinning like an idiot. Her damn voice even had the nerve to be hoarse from their night together.

"I need to go, Ridge." She giggled.

God, when had she giggled so much? Who was this woman? She barely recognized herself. His warm breath blew on her neck as he nuzzled his face against her skin. A bulge rested along her bottom.

She inhaled sharply and tried to ignore it. She had to report to work today, and the man was acting like she didn't have a job.

"But what if I don't want you to?" he replied.

He nipped at her skin, and she moaned. The man had explored her body all night. She'd had barely three hours of sleep the entire night. She was sore in spots she hadn't even known existed. Her pussy had been stretched out in ways it had never been before. She had doubted the man would fit, but he had showed her she could take him perfectly.

Her core clenched at the way his tongue lazily trailed over her skin. The memory of his head buried between her thighs would be forever etched in her brain.

"I have to go to work." She pulled her jeans up and got them buttoned. She still had to put her shirt on, but a certain muscular cowboy was keeping her hostage at the moment.

Did she really want to go to work? To be out in the sun, around cattle and other men who would be sweating just as bad as she would be?

Hell no.

She'd rather remain here with Ridge and have an encore of last night's performance.

"I do know your boss. I can make a call." He lifted his head and dropped a kiss on her cheek.

"You are not calling your father and telling him nothing." She whirled around and pressed a finger to his bare chest. There was no way in hell Ridge was telling his father that she couldn't come to work. That would be embarrassing. What would Andy think if he knew she'd slept with his son? She didn't want anyone getting the wrong thoughts about her.

"I'm just playing. I wouldn't do that." He cupped her face and stared down at her. His smile was gone, and this was the serious side of him. He may be relaxed and joke a lot, but he apparently knew when it was time to be serious. "I wouldn't want you to be uncomfortable in any way around my family."

"It's not that. I like your dad and even your brother. I just don't want anyone else thinking I'm sleeping with you for ulterior reasons," she admitted.

Been there. Done that. But what happened between her and Theo wasn't consensual. But to hear his side of the story, she'd wanted his advances, which was an absolute lie. She hadn't asked to be held down. She hadn't asked for him to rip her dress—

She closed her eyes and pushed that night away from the forefront of her mind. Not here with Ridge.

Ridge was nothing like Theo.

"I get it. I do, but I'm not going to hide my feelings for you from no one." His thumb gently caressed her skin. His eyes darkened into something she'd never seen before. "If someone says anything to you, come to me. I'll handle it."

A shiver went through her. She'd never seen this from Ridge. Maybe there was more to him than what he allowed everyone to see. At that exact moment, the expression in his eyes looked familiar.

His brother.

Even though the two were complete opposites, at the moment, she saw the same darkness his brother carried in Ridge's eyes.

"I can take care of myself," she said softly.

He tightened his hold on her face. It wasn't painful, but that darkness clouded his eyes even more.

"I'm serious, Melah. You are not alone. You don't have to take care of yourself. I'm here with you." He dropped a kiss to her lips, and when he lifted his head, that look in his eyes was gone.

The Ridge she'd come to know was back. She blinked. Had she imagined it?

"Okay." She leaned into him and rested her forehead on his chest. This man knew what she needed in the short time they had been together. It was like the weight was floating from her shoulders. She inhaled his warm scent, which relaxed her. She raised her head and smiled. "I still have to go."

She pushed off him, and he finally released her. She grabbed her shirt and threw it on. Last night Ridge had never got around to grilling. He'd stuck the food in the fridge, tossed her over his shoulder, and they'd ended up in the bedroom.

Her stomach released a growl. She'd get something to eat after a shower before she went out on the ranch for her shift. Who'd have thought the bag she'd packed would come in handy. It had been a little presumptive to think she might spend the night. She was sure when she got back to the bunkhouse that she was going to have to say something to Aimee about her whereabouts.

She zipped up her bag and found him waiting for her by the doorway.

"Got everything?" he asked.

"I think so."

He pushed off the doorjamb and picked up her bag. He took her hand in his and guided them down to the first level. She'd had a quick tour of it last night when she'd arrived. It was a grand home that called to her. She glanced around and could see where she could add a few details. She'd love to put a—

What the hell was she doing?

One night here and she was already thinking of redecorating it?

She shook her head and followed him to the front door. They went outside and down the porch. They arrived at her vehicle, and he tossed her bag in the backseat. It wasn't a far drive to the bunkhouse. He slammed the door shut and turned to her. He leaned back against the car and kept her in the cradle of his embrace. He'd only thrown on shorts as she'd gotten dressed.

"What time are you working until?" he asked.

"Not sure." She shrugged. Some days she had a set time she knew when she'd be getting off, some days she didn't know until she was sent home by Buck. There was always plenty to do on a ranch. She loved the hard manual work that was part of being a hand.

"Why don't I officially cook for us tonight. Faith is on call today, so I don't need to work late. I'll fire up the grill again and have the food ready for you whenever you get off." There was a twinkle in his eyes.

"Will food be the only thing ready for me?" She

arched an eyebrow. She couldn't help but tease him. His bulge pressed into her stomach. She leaned into him and entwined her fingers together at the base of his neck. He was so much taller than her that she had to rise on her tippy toes to do so.

He grinned and tightened his hold on her.

"You never know. Just come by and you'll have to see." Ridge leaned down and took her lips in a soft kiss.

How was she to leave this man and go to work when he pulled moves like this? One moment, he was soft and sensual with her, the next commanding of her body in ways that left her breathless.

"I have to go, Ridge." Her lips brushed his as she spoke. She smiled at him. If she didn't stand firm with him, he'd have her naked and screaming his name again. Butterflies in her stomach fluttered at the image that came to mind. She reached behind her and undid his hands to free herself.

"Will you stop by, or do I need to come and get you?" He leveled her with a heated gaze.

Her breath caught in her throat as she took a step back from him. "I'll text you when I know I'll be getting off."

He nodded and opened her car door for her. He waved her in. She ducked under his arm but didn't miss the hint of his hand brushing her ass. She laughed and hopped in her car.

"Hey! What was that?"

"Something to hold me over until you come back to me." He shut the door and tossed her a wink.

She hit the engine button for her car, and it roared to life. She, again, couldn't erase the silly grin from her lips. She gave him a wave and threw the car in drive. She tightened her grip on the steering wheel and drove away. Her gaze drifted to the rearview mirror and took in his form. He watched her leave.

For some reason, a pain lanced acrossed her heart as the distance between them grew. She sighed and focused back on the dirt road. She had to get her mind together for work. This was a dangerous job, and she could get hurt if she didn't concentrate.

The trip home didn't take long. She parked her car and got out. She snagged her bag and headed inside. She didn't see any signs of Aimee, which was a relief. She didn't want to face her at the moment. Not that she had to tell her anything, but they had an unspoken agreement to look out for one another.

Melah went into her room and dropped her bag on the bed. She paused, a realization hitting her.

In the few hours she'd slept at Ridge's, she hadn't had any nightmares. She'd slept soundly.

Was that all it took?

Get your world rocked by a handsome veterinarian then all of the nightmares will stay away?

She was sore in some places, and she was sure it would be worse come later, but overall, she felt damn good.

She glanced at her phone. She had to be at work in a little over an hour. She had time to grab her shower and a protein bar for breakfast. She'd just make sure she'd stop by for Ms. Bee's lunch later. That would fill her up enough until dinner at Ridge's.

Plan in place, she removed her clothes and grabbed her towel. She wrapped it around herself and walked into the shower room. She took her phone with her so she could listen to music while she washed up.

The shower room had a few private stalls for one to bathe. She caught sight of herself in the mirror and grimaced. She was going to have to quickly wash her hair. After the swim yesterday, she looked like a drowned rat. How did Ridge find her desirable looking like this? That man needed to have his brain checked out.

With music playing from her phone on a ledge out of the way, it didn't take her long to wash herself from head to toe. Once she felt squeaky clean, she shut off the water and reached for her towel. She covered her body with it and picked up another to wrap her hair.

"Someone's in a good mood," Aimee said, breezing into the shower room. She snagged her shower caddy and went over to one of the sinks. She switched on the water and reached for her toothbrush.

"I am." Melah turned her back to Aimee to hide her smile. That damn grin was back. She went over and collected her caddy and phone. The music was still playing at full blast. She set her stuff down on the sink.

"Did it have something to do with you not coming home last night?" Aimee shot her a look.

Melah refused to make eye contact with her. There was no hiding her smile now.

"Maybe..." She snagged her toothbrush and brushed her teeth so she wouldn't have to respond to any more of Aimee's questions. She wasn't even sure she wanted to share any details about her and Ridge. She didn't know what the relationship was between them, but whatever it was felt too personal to share.

"I'm glad you enjoyed yourself and are smiling. Ridge seems to be a good guy." Aimee smiled at her and finished up at the sink. She tossed Melah a wink then made for the showers.

Melah's face warmed. Well, it would seem Aimee had put two and two together.

She had stored her blow dryer beneath the sink. The one thing that made it easier with living in the bunkhouse with only one other woman, there was plenty of room for their items to be spread out. She dried her hair, glanced at it, and decided on two braids. That way, if the sun was beaming down on her, she could toss on a hat to shield her from the warm rays.

She applied some of her favorite products to her hair and scalp before parting it down the middle. The twin braids didn't take long. She cleaned up the sink where she had been working. Aimee had left the shower room a few minutes ago. She, too, had to report at the same time as Melah.

Satisfied with the way her hair came out, she put all of her stuff away, snagged her phone, and went back into her room. She held on to the towel that had suddenly loosened as she made her way to her room. She arrived at the door and froze in place. A chill went through her.

All of the drawers in the dresser were left wide open. Her clothing tossed everywhere. Her bedding had been thrown on the floor. Her eyes immediately went to the safe she'd had installed underneath her bed. She dashed into the room and put her finger over the biometric key. A click sounded, alerting that it was open. She pried it apart, took out her Glock, and flicked off the safety as she kept it loaded.

Who the fuck had been in her room?

"Aimee!" she hollered. She stalked back to door and kept her finger off the trigger. One of the first things she'd learned when handling a gun: *Don't put your finger on the trigger unless you are ready to pull it.* At the moment, she didn't want to accidentally shoot Aimee. Her nerves were frazzled at the fact that someone had invaded her personal space. She glanced down the hallway and didn't see anyone.

"What's wrong?" Aimee came flying out of her room next door. She had a weapon in her hand, too. She must have picked up on the panic in Melah's voice. She had a sports bra on and a pair of unbuttoned jeans.

"Someone has been in my room." Melah used her gun to point back in her room. She held on to her towel with her free hand to keep it from falling off.

Aimee brushed past her and stood in the doorway.

"Son of a bitch," she muttered.

She turned to Melah who shook her head.

"I didn't even open my drawers when I came home. I removed my clothes and went straight into the shower room," Melah said.

"Let's check the rest of the house. We have to notify Andy and Buck." Aimee raised her gun and aimed it true. The house wasn't that big. There was the common area, kitchen, dining space, and a laundry room for the hands. The private bedrooms and the shower room with toilet rooms were housed in the same area.

Melah and Aimee cleared the entire house in under three minutes. There was no one in it but them.

Aimee walked over to front door and jiggled the handle. It was locked. Melah's heart raced. Who the hell would sneak in and rifle through her shit?

"Throw some clothes on and check to see if anything's missing. I'm calling Buck." Aimee strode away and went down the hall where their bedrooms were located.

Melah glanced around the common area at the large couches, a fireplace, and a television for the hands to watch when relaxing after work.

The hairs on the back of her neck were erect.

Suddenly, somewhere that was supposed to be a

safe haven for her was ruined. She glanced down at her faithful weapon and knew from this moment on, she wasn't going to go anywhere without it.

Her gut had never led her astray when she was deployed, and she was going to listen to it now.

She gripped the gun tight and went to her room. Whoever had come into her private domain while she was gone, better not try it while she was here. They would not walk away the next time.

She guaranteed that.

Chapter Twelve

"We'll alert everyone to what happened," Buck said. The elder cowboy's scowl was embedded in his face. He stepped out of the women's house and turned to eye the building.

"How do we know someone on the ranch didn't do this?" Aimee asked.

"They better not have. We have good men here. I'm not going to go around blaming anyone unless we have proof." He rested his hands on his waist. His gaze cut to Melah. "We'll call the police and file a report. You're sure nothing is missing?"

"No. Nothing was missing." Melah folded her arms.

After Aimee had placed the call to Buck, the

lead hand had showed up almost immediately. It shook her to her core that someone had invaded her space. She wondered how the person had got in without either her or Aimee noticing. Had she left the door unlocked when she'd come in and they'd locked it on their way out?

"I'm going to tell you now, anyone coming in this building without announcing themselves will get their ass shot," Aimee warned.

"Same," Melah agreed.

By the time Buck had arrived, Melah was fully dressed, and she even had on her thigh holster that she loved. The sense of having someone going through her personal items gave her a bad taste in her mouth.

"I don't blame you gals at all. Make sure you call me as soon as you do shoot whatever fucker— I mean asshole—idiot who comes unannounced," Buck said, stumbling over his words. He may be a hardened rancher, but he still tried to be a gentleman around women.

Another truck rolled up to the house and parked. Melah stiffened for a moment, then relaxed when she saw the driver.

It was Andy.

He cut the engine to his pickup truck and slid

out. The elder Harvey man ambled over to them, and in his gaze, she immediately saw Draven and Ridge. There was no doubt in her mind who their father was. His hair was grayed, and he was still physically fit for his age. At the moment, his gaze landed on her. It dropped down to her weapon on her thigh. Something clouded over in his gaze.

"Everyone all right?" He came to stand by Buck who immediately brought him up to speed.

Buck had called him and told him something urgent had happened at their bunkhouse before he had arrived.

"If you ladies don't feel safe tonight, you are more than welcome to stay at the main house. We have a few guest bedrooms that family use when they visit," Andy said.

"There won't be a need," Aimee said. "I'm not going to lose any sleep. They can try to come in again if they want to."

The woman's voice hardened, and Melah felt the same emotions as the Air Force veteran. She'd be sleeping with her gun under her pillow tonight.

"I'm good, too, but thanks," Melah said.

"Buck is going to have a deputy out here to file a report. No matter what happens, we need to have this documented. Hopefully it was some silly kid prank or something," Andy said, but he didn't look too convinced of his own feeble excuse.

"Kids don't come in then leave without a trace or a sound," Aimee muttered.

"Well, we'll be changing the locks. We'll give the house a once-over to make sure there's no easy way into it." Andy folded his arms.

The way he zeroed in on her made her think of Ridge. Should she call him and tell him? She brushed off that thought. She didn't want him worried or leaving work.

Plus...he wasn't really her man.

They'd had sex. He'd said he wanted what she had to offer, but at the moment she didn't know what she had to offer besides a few fun nights together.

No, there wasn't a need to call him.

Andy and Buck entered the house, speaking in low, even tones.

Aimee turned to her with a frown. "You sure you're good?"

"As ever. It's just weird that they went in my room only and not yours," Melah said.

"Maybe I scared them off. I left the shower room before you."

That did make sense. Melah had stayed in the shower room and worked on her hair. Aimee had jumped in and out quick since they had to be at work.

"Yeah. Too bad you didn't see them," Melah said.

They walked toward the house and went inside. Andy and Buck were walking around the common area checking out the windows.

"I'll have everything taken care of by the end of the day, ladies. Don't worry. This won't happen again. I'll even have some cameras installed, too, and make sure the lights are bright at night," Andy said.

Melah appreciated everything he was doing. He obviously took their safety seriously and didn't brush it off. He was a good man and cared for every person who came to work at the ranch. She'd heard nice things about him through the grapevine. He was a man of his word, and whatever he promised, he always followed through.

"We're going to wait outside for the deputy. They shouldn't be too much longer." Andy motioned to Melah. "Can we speak with you for a moment, Melah?"

"Um, yeah. Sure." She glanced at Aimee who arched an eyebrow at her. She shook her head and followed behind Andy and Buck.

They stepped back outside and walked over to

Andy's truck. He turned and leaned back against his vehicle.

"What's going on, boss?"

"You don't think this could be that fella you had issues with when you were enlisted, do you?" he asked.

She stiffened. Well, he certainly didn't beat around the bush. She glanced away from him and blew out a shaky breath. There was no need for her to lie or try to hide anything from him.

"Listen, we know this is a sore subject, but we do backgrounds on everyone who comes through the Silver Creek Ranch. We want to know who'll be working here," Buck said.

"I understand. I just don't know the answer to the question. I don't think Theo is out of prison." Just saying his name had her feeling nauseated. She ran a palm along her face and saw that her hand was trembling. She clenched it into a fist. She was told that she'd be notified if he was released from prison.

"I'm not trying to be in your business, Melah, but if he's here, you need to tell us immediately." Andy narrowed his gaze on her.

She held her breath, waiting to hear what he was going to say. Would she have to leave to keep the peace on the ranch? She was just liking it here, and if she had to pack up and go, she truly didn't know what her next step would be.

"You are a good woman. Dependable, and everyone appears to enjoy your company, and you are Army. You are one of us, and we protect our own here."

"We sure as fuck do," Buck growled. He took off his hat and ran his fingers through his graying hair. His eyes crinkled in the corners as a deep chuckle escaped him. "You couldn't be more safer on the Silver Creek than anywhere else."

She gave a nod. Her heart swelled at their words. She blinked back tears and glanced away again. She didn't know what was going on with her, but it must be something in the air.

"Thanks. It means the world to me. I like the ranch. It's given me so much in my short time here," she admitted. She thought of all the guys she had gotten to know and worked with. They were all working through shit like she was.

"Well, you know there's no rush for you to leave. There's always work to be done." Andy smiled.

She barked a laugh. Boy, did she know that. With a ranch this size, she was surprised anyone was allowed to go home and get sleep.

"And then today, I go and be late to work," she joked.

"Don't worry about it. I hear your boss is a big softie," Buck said.

"Say what now?" Andy sputtered.

A police SUV made its way down the dirt road toward them. Melah may have felt better at the moment, but her thoughts were now racing.

Was it Theo?

It couldn't be. Why would he seek her out?

She remembered that day in court as they'd taken him away. He had turned toward her and stared at her with the most menacing glare. According to him, she'd ruined his career. His life.

"You bitch!" he screamed. Theo's dark hair fell forward in his face.

The bailiffs gripped him and dragged him toward the door.

"Everything is going to be all right," her father said. Through the entire trial, he'd been by her side. He took her hand in his and brought her to him, wrapping an arm around her shoulders. "He can't hurt you any longer, baby girl."

"I know, Dad," she whispered.

She held Theo's gaze until he disappeared behind the doors. She wasn't going to back down from him.

Not ever again. He'd thought he'd intimidate her through the entire trial, but he'd failed.

Melah blinked and came back to the present. The sheriff's vehicle stopped. Buck walked over to it and met the officer who stepped from the truck. She inhaled sharply, prepared to answer all of his questions.

If this was Theo, he was going to wish he'd forgotten her.

* * *

"What they calling a meeting for?" Trent muttered, coming to stand next to Melah.

She already knew what it was for, but she shrugged. Andy and Buck had sent out a message to all the hands who were working that day to stop at the barn for an important meeting before they left.

She eyed the group of about thirty who gathered around. Everyone had the look of working a hard day. It had been a long one. Melah would love to take a soak in a hot bath, but unfortunately, the bunkhouse only had showers. Today, she had brought Daisy out and she had done amazing on her foot. There was no limp, and she'd jumped right into work when it was time to move cattle to another area.

"We aren't going to keep you. We know today was hard, and I'm sure you're ready to get the hell up out of here," Buck said.

Chuckles went around the group. Some of the hands were permeant employees, but most were like her and Aimee. Former servicemen and women who needed help. She eyed them and saw a few men from her therapy group. Seeing their faces reminded her that they had another session scheduled for tomorrow. She wasn't going to miss it.

"Is something wrong, boss man?" a thick drawl called out from the back of the crowd.

"We just want to alert everyone that there has been a security breach at the women's bunkhouse. Now I'm not going to go into too many details unless the ladies want to share, but someone broke into their house," Andy announced.

Silence fell across the group. Where there had been small, quiet conversations going on before, they all ceased. Tension rose in the air.

"Was anything stolen?" Ethan's gaze landed on her through the throng of people.

Aimee was standing not too far behind her.

"No, nothing was stolen." Melah tilted her chin upward. She refused to show weakness. She didn't know every person who worked the ranch, but if

Andy and Buck believed it had to be someone from the outside, then she'd listen to them. "But I promise you, this will be the last time they enter our house unannounced."

"They sure as shit won't be walking out," Aimee chimed in.

Tense chuckles went around at her comment.

But she wasn't joking, and neither was Melah.

Melah was a deadly shot. She had earned plenty of awards for her marksmanship, and even deployed, her shot always hit its mark.

"If you ladies need anything, don't hesitate to call," Trent said.

In her short time on the ranch, she had already felt Trent would be a person she could call a friend. She jerked her head in a nod at his offer.

"Want some of us to do walk throughs at night for the next couple of days?" someone else offered.

Other suggestions were made, and it warmed Melah's heart. Andy's words came back to her.

You are one of us, and we protect our own here.

"What do you think?" Aimee asked. She came to stand next to Melah.

She didn't have an issue with any of the guys driving by at night to ensure everything was safe and sound for them.

"I'm good with it if you are," she said.

"A few days should be fine, just to ensure whoever this fucker is don't come back," Aimee announced.

"Don't worry about wondering if we'll lose sleep." Trent smirked. He ran fingers through his hair. "I can't even remember the last time I got a full night's rest."

"Same," other men muttered.

"Well, I appreciate it," Melah said.

Some of the guys got together and started coming up with a plan of patrolling.

Andy and Buck shouted out other announcements before releasing those who wanted to leave. The hairs on the back of Melah's neck rose. She glanced over her shoulder, feeling as if someone was watching her. She glanced around, and her gaze met a familiar set of blue eyes.

Ridge.

And he was pissed. He pushed off the side of the barn and stalked toward her. Melah swallowed hard and watched him. Another figure trailed behind him who had an inch on him in height and wider.

Draven.

Melah felt like a deer caught in headlights as the Harvey brothers made their way to her. She at first thought about turning around and scurrying away, but she was no coward. She could handle Ridge and him being upset.

Draven, on the other hand, with his dark, threatening look, she was ready to sprint away from that man. No amount of military training would prepare her to face him in a dark alley.

"Ridge," she said.

He stopped in front of her. She had never seen him look like this.

He reached for her and cupped her face in his hand.

"Why didn't you call me?" he growled.

Draven silently came to stand next to them. His gaze flicked back and forth between them. Something dawned in his eyes. He remained quiet and folded his arms.

"What are you talking about?" She glanced around, and all eyes were on them.

He tightened his hold on her.

"When this happened, why didn't you call me?" Ridge demanded. His chest was rising and falling fast. There was a slight flush to his skin. He glared at her.

"Everything happened so fast. Aimee called

Buck who then called your dad. Everything was taken care of," she explained.

But he shook his head and brought her closer to him. If there was any question on whether or not there was something going on between them, it was now answered for the entire ranch to know.

"And you didn't think to call me?" he asked.

She inhaled sharply and rested a hand on his chest to try to calm him down. "Can we talk about this in private?"

He blinked as if forgetting they had an audience. He jerked his head in a nod and took her by the hand. He spun on his heels and tugged her behind him, leading her away.

Her heart raced. Ridge was upset because she hadn't called him. With the way he gripped her hand, she didn't utter a word. She was left speechless by him. They arrived at his truck that was parked out front with Draven who'd remained a few steps behind them.

Ridge spun on her and faced her again.

"Now tell me everything."

Chapter Thirteen

Ridge felt his brother's eyes on him, but he couldn't look at him. All he could see was Melah who had a confused expression in her eyes. Hearing that someone had broken into the women's bunkhouse while she'd been in the shower had him seeing red. Something didn't sit right with him. There had never been any incidents like this on the ranch. Who would be bold enough to come on their property and then vandalize a building?

Even though Melah had confirmed nothing had been taken, he could tell it was directed at her. Only her room? Something was going on, and he wanted her to tell him everything.

"Now, I want to know what is really going on. You know something," he said through gritted teeth.

Draven moved over to the front of his truck and leaned back as if to appear casual, but Ridge knew his brother. He may not be looking at them, but he was listening to every word.

"There's not much more than what we told the deputy. My room was ransacked and nothing was missing. We don't even know how they got in. The doors were locked when we checked," she said.

He released her hand for fear of hurting her. He lifted his hat and raked his fingers through his hair.

"So you don't know who could have done this?" He was trying to get himself under control. Being around her brought out the protective nature in him. He wanted to be the one she turned to. He wanted to be the one to shield her from the world. She may be a military woman, but that didn't mean she wouldn't need someone to have her back. "There's a reason you're carrying your gun now. You haven't done this before."

She glanced down at her holster on her thigh. He had been shocked at first when he'd arrived at the group and saw she had a gun on her. It wasn't uncommon to carry a rifle when dealing with predators coming onto the ranch and trying to take out a calf or smaller animals.

"I mean, I suspected someone, but I seriously doubt it was him." She blew out a shaky breath and folded her arms.

She took a few steps away from him, and that was too far. He reached for her and gently took her arm and turned her back to him.

"What do you mean?" he asked softly. He didn't want to scare her away and have her keep anything from him. This thing between them was moving fast, but he didn't care. He was in for the ride and wanted her. Whatever he had to do to make her stay, he was willing to do.

He needed her.

Ridge swallowed hard. Melah's brown-eyed gaze landed on him, and the air in his lungs rushed out. A weight settled on his heart, and it was then he realized his heart belonged to her.

"There was a reason I left the military when I did." She hesitated.

She blinked, and her muscles stiffened underneath his touch. He released her arm and took her hand in his.

"I'm listening. There is no judgement here. Not from me—"

"Or me," Draven cut in. He tossed them a look over his shoulder before going back to staring out at the landscape.

Ridge already knew he and his brother were going to have a conversation. If Melah meant something to Ridge, then already Draven would accept her.

Her eyes cast down to the ground. He tipped her chin up so she could see he was open and willing to listen to whatever it was. There had always been something hidden in her eyes. Something haunted her—hell, half the vets who came to Silver Creek had something weighing them down. Demons chased them all. But whatever it was that bothered her, he wanted to take it away from her.

"I was raped by my sergeant," she whispered.

Ridge's heart stopped. Pain, embarrassment, and shame flooded her eyes. She tried to look away from him, but he held her steady. This wasn't the first time he'd heard of something like this happening in the military. Most times it was covered up and brushed off.

"I'm so sorry," he said.

She studied him for a moment as if to see if his opinion about her had changed.

It hadn't.

Hearing what had happened to her only made him want to do bodily damage to whoever the fucker was who'd done such a horrid thing to her.

"You don't need to apologize." She sniffed.

She blinked, and he saw a strength in her come to the forefront.

"I filed a formal complaint. Charges were brought up against him. He was arrested. There was a trial, and he was sent away to prison."

"Good." The word fell from his lips automatically. Hearing this just proved how strong she was. Not many women pushed forward to get justice from the person who'd assaulted them. Melah was a special woman.

"They tried to break me, you know. Everyone tried to get me to drop the charges. Told me I would ruin his career." A sarcastic chuckle fell from her lips.

He released her face but still didn't want to stop touching her.

She reached up and brushed a few rogue strands of her hair from her face. "But no one talked about how his actions ruined mine. I lost everything. The man I was supposed to marry, who claimed to love me, didn't believe me. He accused me of lying and using the charges as a way to hide an affair between me and Theo."

Now there were two men on Ridge's shit list. Whoever the man she had been engaged to was, didn't deserve her. How could he not believe her if she'd said another had raped her?

"Melah," he murmured.

But she held up a hand and shook her head. She took a few steps back from him.

"No, you wanted to know everything, so I'm going to just say it. My ex-fiancé accused me of cheating after I told him I was raped. I was held down, taken against my will, but no. He believed everything he heard from the rumor mill, people trying to discredit me, but not me. The trial exposed everything about me. My father had to listen to the details of Theo attacking me, forcing himself on me, the details from the hospital visit —they embarrassed me, dragged up every sexual ordeal I'd ever had just to try to prove that Theo was innocent and that I wanted him to do those things to me. But everyone on that damn base knew he wasn't innocent. I wasn't the first woman he'd assaulted. I was the only one brave enough to come forward." By this time, tears were streaming down her face. The pain in her voice and in her eyes was enough to crush a man.

Ridge reached for her and brought her into his embrace. Her body shook from the sobs coming from her. He held her tight and looked over her shoulder. He was sure the dark expression on his brother's face was mirrored on his.

Ridge wanted to hurt someone bad for causing this pain in his woman. He actually hoped the burglar was this Theo character. A chilling feeling he hadn't felt in years claimed him. If he ever did come across Theo, he guaranteed the other man wouldn't be walking away.

"You're safe here." He brought his lips to her temple and kissed her skin.

She was no longer going to have to carry the burden of this pain all by herself. She may not realize it now, but this was where she belonged. He was going to prove that without a doubt his arms were where she needed to be—forever.

Her sobs finally subsided. His shirt was balled up into her tiny fists. She rested her forehead on his chest, and a tremor snaked through her.

"Is he still in prison?" Draven asked.

"For all I know, he's supposed to be." She lifted her head from Ridge's chest. She wiped her face with the back of her hand. Her eyes were slightly swollen.

"I have a few contacts I can reach out to. I need

to know his entire name and I can confirm whether or not he's been released," Draven said.

His brother slid his phone from his back jean pocket. The elder Harvey sibling had served for way longer than Ridge had. Draven was a legend. His former team was special ops, and there was much that Draven couldn't speak about, but if he said he still had people he could reach out to, Ridge was certain Draven could have information in a manner of minutes.

"Theo English is his full name," she said softly.

Ridge reached for her hand and entwined their fingers together. Draven asked a few more questions before confirming he had all he needed.

"This won't take long. I'll let you know what I find." Draven gave them a nod and walked off, leaving the two of them alone.

Ridge waited until his brother had disappeared around the barn before he turned his attention back on Melah.

They stood in silence staring at each other.

"I come with a lot of baggage," she admitted.

He shrugged and tugged her to him. Hearing the horror of what had happened to her didn't scare him off. It just proved she was a strong woman who he was falling in love with and he'd do anything to help her. He didn't like seeing her like this.

"Is that supposed to scare me off?" he asked softly. He tilted her chin back and gazed into her eyes. He wanted to ensure she saw all of his feelings for her. It was too soon to drop the 'L word', but he knew he was falling for her. This woman already owned his heart, and after the night they'd shared together, he was ready to give it to her.

"I don't know."

He lowered his head slightly and pressed his lips to hers. She parted hers immediately and welcomed him. She had been through so much, and he wanted to prove to her that he found her desirable and wasn't going to run away because of a past she had no control over.

Her arms came up to wrap around his neck. He slid his hands down to her lower back and held her to him. He slowly broke the kiss and peppered small kisses to her lips.

"I'm not going anywhere, Melah Battle. Now, you're going to pack your stuff and come stay at my house."

"I am not." She tried to pull away from him, but he held her to him firmly. "I'm not running away from someone. We don't even know who did this. For all we know it could be some punk kids playing a prank—a stupid one—but a prank nonetheless."

"Does it matter? I need to know that you're safe at all times." He wasn't going to argue with her on this. He'd do what he needed to ensure she was safe and secure.

"I'll be fine. The guys have volunteered to patrol for a few nights to make sure whoever it was doesn't come back."

She rolled her eyes and tried to push him away, but he didn't budge. He was being serious. The only way he could keep her safe was to have her in his house.

She glanced at him again and exhaled. "I can't just up and move in with you, Ridge."

"Why not?" he demanded to know.

Everyone on the ranch now knew they were together. He hadn't been thinking at the meeting. He'd had tunnel vision and only saw Melah as they'd spoken about what had transpired in the bunkhouse.

"Because...um, I don't know. I just know I can't move in with you," she exclaimed.

"Then I'm going to stay with you. Let me run up to my house and grab a bag," he said.

If she wasn't going to come to him, then he'd stay with her. It didn't sit right with him that someone had been in the house when she'd been vulnerable. Anything could have happened to her.

"What? No, you are not going to stay in the bunkhouse. You have an entire house here on the ranch—"

"That you can stay at! Aimee can come, too."

"She already said she's not leaving, and I'm not abandoning her there to be alone." Melah folded her arms.

There was a stubborn tilt to her chin when she met his gaze. There was no reasoning with Melah, he could clearly see that.

"Fine." Ridge exhaled. He knew when he was fighting a losing battle. He ran a hand along his face and nodded. "If you're sure you will be okay, then I'll trust your judgement."

"Aimee and I will be fine. I promise you, the next time someone enters the house uninvited, they will be leaving in a body bag."

Ridge's cock immediately stiffened. His woman was no damsel in distress, and that was what attracted him to her the most. He stepped forward and gripped the back of her neck. His lips curved up as he stared down at her.

"And what if a certain person kidnapped you for

a few hours and took you back to his house? What would happen to him?" he growled.

She leaned toward him, erasing the distance between their bodies. Her curvy frame fit his perfectly.

"The brave man better at least let me shower first since I've been working all day or he might get hurt. After that, he can take me away for a few hours since this certain person promised me dinner tonight." Her grin was wide, and she stared up at him.

Ridge barked a laugh. Hell, he didn't care that she'd been working all day. He wanted her just as she was. He'd worked a ranch his entire life, but he knew he'd better concede.

"Very well then. I'll take you home for a quick shower, then I'll make good on my promise."

Chapter Fourteen

"This was so good." Melah patted her stomach and sat back in her chair.

As promised, Ridge had taken her home so she could shower. She'd jumped in quick to wash the long day from her skin. He'd waited in the common area speaking with Aimee while she'd gotten ready. With the promise that she'd be back later that night, they'd left.

"I'm glad you enjoyed it." He reached for his longneck bottle and took a swig from it.

They'd arrived at his house where he'd grilled out on the deck. They were currently sitting at the small dining table on the deck enjoying the warm weather. Melah was in love with the home. Having a large pond and nature literally at the back door was an amazing thing to have.

She could get used to it.

"I did. It's so relaxing out here." She glanced at the sight of a hawk flying. Its wingspan was spread out wide as it glided through the air. One thing she loved about South Dakota was the open skies and land. The air alone was different. She inhaled and swore it was fresher than where she'd grown up.

"If you want, I have dessert in the house." He stood and began clearing the table.

She pushed back and reached for her plate.

He motioned for her to hand it to him. "I've got it. You can sit out here longer while I start the dishwasher."

"Absolutely not. If you cooked, then I clean." She ignored his outstretched hand and picked up her dirty dishes. She was never one to sit down while someone else did things for her. Pierce had not been able to boil water. It was a wonder he was able to survive on his own. It was nice to think she had a man who could cook and was willing to clean. She turned to the house and froze for a second.

She had a who?

Was there any reason for her to keep fighting

this? Ridge had made it clear he wanted her. She was here now. For how long, she didn't know.

She bit her lip and continued on to the door. Ridge arrived before her and opened it. The warmth in his eyes set off a chain reaction in her body. Her breath caught in her throat, her nipples hardened and pushed at her bra, and the butterflies in her stomach fluttered overtime.

No, there was no fighting this. She tried to think of not being with Ridge, or him moving on, and she immediately wanted to do damage to whatever woman tried to catch his eye.

Ridge was her man.

"Thanks." She smiled and ducked underneath his arm and went inside. She went over to the sink and placed the dishes down and turned the water on.

"You do not have to do this. You are a guest." He set his down in the sink next to hers and opened the dishwasher.

"You cooked. I clean." She rinsed off her plate and elbowed him to move out of her way.

He barked a laugh and held up his hands. He backed away from her.

"Fine." He moved over and snagged his beer, tilted it back, and finished it off.

She worked in silence and quickly loaded the

dishwasher up. Their conversation turned to his work. She was always curious to hear about his day. It was interesting to hear him speak of his patients as if they were humans. Anyone could see how much he truly loved what he did. From scheduled procedures, checkups to emergency surgeries, he'd had a busy few hours. Once she was done with cleaning, she went over to the fridge and took out a bottle of water. Ridge fell quiet. She turned and found his gaze on her.

"What?" She twisted open the bottle and took a swig of water then replaced the cap. She tilted her head and met his eyes as he studied her.

"I like seeing you here," he admitted.

"In your kitchen?" She arched an eyebrow at him. She walked around the island and came to stand before him.

He chuckled and shook his head.

"In my home," he replied softly.

He took the bottle from her and set it on the counter. He reached for her and lifted her. He sat her on the island. Melah's legs automatically parted to allow him to stand between them. She inhaled sharply at their closeness. His hands ran along her bare legs. A tremor snuck through her at the feeling of his hands on her skin.

She had thrown on a soft yellow summer dress and sandals after she'd gotten out of the shower. She had left her hair in twin braids. She'd fixed it up a little because it had felt good to keep her hair off her neck with the heatwave they were experiencing.

"What about me being here?" she whispered. She rested her hands on his shoulders. Sitting on the island allowed them to be eye level with each other. She memorized the clearness of his blue eyes, the stubble on his jawline, and his perfect white teeth as he smiled at her. His muscles underneath her touch were relaxed.

His hands slipped underneath the edge of her dress. "You belong here."

"And you know this only after me being here a couple of times already?" She arched an eyebrow at him again and slipped a hand up along the column of his neck to the new growth of a beard on his face. She loved the feeling of the prickliness of the short hairs on her palm. She ran her thumb along his bottom lip. "I'm just a woman visiting."

"It could be more than visiting." He gripped her thighs tight and moved one of his hands up to her face and held her in place. He lowered his head. His lips brushed hers in the softest kiss.

Melah's breath caught in her throat. This man

did not beat around the bush when it came to sharing what he was thinking. What was between them was moving faster than a bullet train, and at the moment, she didn't want to get off.

"Ridge, we just met," she whispered. It was a feeble excuse, but it was the truth. A few weeks ago, she'd only known of him. Now, she'd slept with him already and was clearly falling for him.

"And? What is that supposed to mean? I know all I need to know about you." He nuzzled his face in the crook of her neck.

She tilted her head to the side to give him access. His devilish tongue slid along her skin. A moan slipped from Melah. Her core clenched with need from the feeling of his hands and his tongue.

"Say you're mine."

"Ridge," she gasped and dove her fingers into his thick hair.

She loved the feeling of his strands. She gripped it tight, and he nipped her gently.

"Say it." His lips brushed along her skin. He pressed hot open-mouthed kisses to her neck while his hands got busy and lifted her dress from underneath her bottom. He bit her again. "Melah."

"I'm yours," she moaned.

It was freeing to have the words spill from her

lips. It was the truth. In the short time they'd been together, she felt owned and possessed by this man. Not in a negative way, but Ridge immediately had her feeling as if she truly belonged to him. He was open with his feelings, made her feel wanted, was ready to protect her—everything she had never felt before in her previous relationships.

Fuck it.

She was his and he was hers. This was something she was damn certain of. Everything else, she'd figure out in the future. One day at a time was going to be her new motto. And each day, Ridge would be included.

"What about you?" Melah asked.

He pulled away from her and raised her dress over her head. He tossed it down on the floor. The heat that poured from his eyes had her pussy drenched. It was amazing how this man could just look at her and she was primed and ready for him.

"Baby, you had me the first time you smiled at me."

A gasp escaped her just as he swooped down and took her lips in a hard kiss. This wasn't a docile, cute kiss. This was the type of kiss a man gives a woman that left no doubt in her mind of his intentions.

Melah leaned into it, no longer afraid of the unknown.

Because right now, she knew exactly where she stood with him. She may not know what her future held, but at this moment, there was her and Ridge.

He was like an incoming storm. Electricity filled the air between them. She removed his shirt. She slid her hands down his perfectly chiseled chest to his belt. She undid it and moved it out of the way to get to the button of his jeans. His hands were busy removing her bra. The offending material fell from her body to reveal her aching breasts.

"Fuck, you are gorgeous," he murmured. He paused and stared down at her. His hand came to cup one of her mounds. "I hope you know this."

A lump formed in her throat. She couldn't formulate a word. The expression in his blue eyes had her feeling things she was unfamiliar with. He kissed her again before pushing her down on the island. The chill from the surface was welcome against her warm skin. She lifted her hips so he could tug off her panties.

There was no embarrassment at the position she found herself in. Her legs fell open, and a growl rumbled from Ridge when he gazed at her. She was open and exposed to him, but she felt sexy and empowered with the reaction her body drew from him.

"Ridge. I ache for you. I want your mouth here." She reached down between her legs and parted her slick folds to showcase her delicate pearl. She used her finger to roll her sensitive clit.

"What else do you want?" He braced his hands on the counter with his focus on her center.

She smirked at the look of hunger on his face. She played with her clit again and rolled it between two of her fingers. A moan slipped from her from the sensations the move gave her. She slipped her finger farther through her slit and guided it to her opening. She pushed her finger inside and arched her hips to meet it. "I want your dick here."

His audible swallow was the only sound to come from him. She added another finger and repeatedly plunged them as far as she could into her wet channel. Another moan tore from her. She liked having him watch her. She didn't care they were in the kitchen. All that mattered was this man was hungry for her.

He had yet to respond to her.

"Need me to repeat myself?" she gasped.

She couldn't get herself stretched as wide as he could and she couldn't wait to feel that burn she knew that came from his cock breaching her. He had yet to take his eyes off her fucking herself. She withdrew her slippery fingers and moved them to show him exactly what she wanted.

"Your tongue here on my clit. Your dick here in my pussy."

She pushed her fingers back inside and groaned.

Something in Ridge snapped. He trapped her wrist and pulled her hand away from her center. He took her fingers and brought them to his mouth. He licked them completely clean of her wetness. She inhaled sharply, her core clenching. He ensured every drop of her cream was gone from her fingers.

"So fucking good," he murmured then released her wrist.

His eyes had darkened to where they appeared black, and Melah sensed a shift in him. His lips brushed her inner thigh, and she knew in that minute this man truly owned her body. He moved to the other thigh and pressed a kiss to that one. She shook, anticipation building up inside her. She spread herself open for him, waiting for the moment his tongue connected with her swollen bundle of nerves. She entwined her fingers in his hair and tried to guide him to her center.

He growled, "Don't rush me."

She fell back against the counter and cried out in frustration. His lips slowly made their way to her core, and she could have wept. His tongue slid through her entire slit, taking his own taste of her. Melah held on to his head the second his lips closed around her swollen bundle of nerves. She gasped and arched her hips to him.

The man didn't play when it came to feasting on her. He consumed her like a starving man eating his first full meal in weeks. Her cries filled the air while he worked her body. Her legs shook from the sensations coursing through her.

Ridge's tongue and fingers worked her up in the most delicious way. He brought her to the edge of ecstasy but didn't allow her to cross the line. Her begging and pleading went ignored. She rotated her hips to him. Two of his fingers were inside her, thrusting hard while he suckled her clit. She moved in the rhythm of his hand while he fucked her this way.

Melah had a firm grip on his hair. She glanced down at his head between her legs and loved the sight of him where he was.

"Ridge," she gasped.

He rotated his fingers around in a circle and hit the spot inside her that sent her spiraling out of control. She screamed his name, her orgasm overtaking her. It was amazing she didn't tear the hair from his head. She arched upward while her body shook and trembled. Her eyes were squeezed shut, and she rode the waves of intense pleasure that rocked her.

He didn't give her any reprieve. The man was set on owning her body and soul. He continued his welcoming assault on her clit. Her muscles pulsated around his fingers. She shook her head, unable to withstand anymore.

"Please," she gasped. She needed him inside her. She no longer wanted his talented fingers. She needed his thick cock pushing into her. "Ridge. I need you. Please give me your dick."

She may be a proud woman, but she had no problems begging Ridge to fill her up with his big cock.

He released her clit then gave it a kiss. He glanced up at her and licked his lips. That infamous grin of his appeared. "Well, since you asked so nicely."

He lowered his head again and kissed her sensitive clit. He stood straight and reached for his jeans. Melah didn't care what she looked like spread out on his kitchen island. He shoved his jeans down, freeing his engorged member. A moan came from Melah, and she zeroed in on it. She used her weak arms to push up into a sitting position. He kicked his jeans off and reached for her. She went into his arms willingly.

She hopped down from the island. The air escaped her as he twirled her around to bring her back to his chest. His cock rested along her bottom. It was hard and hot, and she couldn't wait to feel him in her. He tapped her ankles with his foot to spread her legs open. He nuzzled her neck. He slowly rubbed himself on her.

"Ridge," she moaned.

"Keep saying my name. I want to hear it," he murmured.

He pushed her forward to brace against the island. He guided the thick mushroomed tip of his member to her opening. He ran it through her slit to gather some of her wetness on it. She whimpered and held still when he paused at her opening. He pushed forward and breached her.

"Oh God," she cried out.

His hands rested on her hip and her neck. She bit her lip, and he fed more of his cock into her. The stretch and burn of her channel sent an electrical current through her body. Once he was buried fully inside her, she finally breathed.

"Fuck. You feel so damn good, Melah."

His large hand tightened on her neck, applying a slight pressure. His other hand gripped her hip, and he withdrew and then sank into her again.

"Don't move."

His words were clipped and strangled. Melah reached down and gripped the edge of the counter. She was never one to listen to orders too well. She rotated her hips, eliciting a curse from Ridge. He withdrew and slammed into her hard. A cry tore from her.

"I told you not to move." He repeated the motion, and this time he kept going.

Melah welcomed each hard thrust. The sounds of their lovemaking took over the kitchen. Ridge continued to pound away into her. He reached a depth that she didn't think was possible.

She chanted his name. Her brain couldn't formulate any other word. She held on for dear life to the counter while he gave her his all. She moved her hips to meet his, and it wasn't long before his grip on her grew painful. The angle of his cock entering her set off another climax for Melah. She cried out while her entire body grew taut. Ridge roared and filled her with streams of his release. His hips jerked a few more times before falling still.

Melah rested her cheek on the cool surface and tried to get control of her breathing. She closed her eyes and inhaled. Her heart pounded. She didn't ever want to move. Ridge was still lodged inside her —she was complete.

Chapter Fifteen

Melah glanced out of her bedroom window and chuckled. It had been a few days since the break-in. She reached for her boots and tugged them on. She shook her head and made her way out of her bedroom. It was early in the morning, and daylight was just breaking. She opened the door to the house and stepped outside. She walked around the building and went into the small wooded area nearby.

"You don't have to sleep out here. We are fine." She paused a few feet away from his little camp he'd been making.

Ridge Harvey was one stubborn man. He pushed off the ground from where he'd been sitting. He raked his fingers through his hair and ambled over to her. The butterflies in her stomach were in overdrive. It was crazy how this man affected her. She held her ground as he arrived in front of her.

"Good morning to you, too." He reached for her and brought her flush to him. He dropped a soft kiss to her lips. "You won't stay at my house, so that means I camp outside yours."

"Trent and the guys have been coming by to make sure all is good. You can sleep in your bed at night."

"Without you there?"

She sighed and leaned into him. He couldn't keep saying stuff like this. He was determined to get what he wanted, and that was her at his place twenty-four seven.

"Ridge, I can't move in with you," she said.

"It's not moving in. It's spending the night, every night." He grinned at her.

She slapped him on the chest and moved away.

"Thats the same damn thing." She glanced at her watch and grimaced. It was almost time for her to report to work. She was sure he was going into the office today, and to think that he'd slept on this hard ground all night had her feeling bad for him.

"Is not." The man had the nerve to laugh. He went over to the sleeping bag and rolled it up.

He began collecting his few items, and it was then she noticed the gun sheathed on a holster on his belt. It made her feel some kind of way that this man was trying to protect her. Maybe she should have invited him in. She'd known when he'd arrived last night. He'd caused enough noise to alert her of his presence, then all had gone silent.

She'd slept all night—again.

Something about having this man near her seemed to keep the nightmares away.

She watched him come toward her again.

"Want to head up to the big house and grab breakfast? I'm sure Bee has food ready," he suggested.

"I can't. I have to clock in soon." She'd love nothing more than to grab some of Bee's cooking. She made a mental note to head over there for lunch today. Bee always had a hot meal ready for the hands on the ranch. "But you go ahead. I'm sure you have a long day today."

"I do. I have some things to do here, so I'm going to start here, then I have other farm calls to do." He tossed his bag onto his shoulder and brought her close to him again. This next kiss was slow and thorough.

Melah gripped his shirt and had to hold on due

to her legs becoming weak. He released her and stared down into her eyes. It was almost as if the man could see into her soul. She exhaled and smiled softly.

"Have a great day today." As much as she wanted to drag this man somewhere to have her way with him, she couldn't. Work was waiting for her. The past few days on the ranch had been smooth. There hadn't been any signs of anyone coming onto the property who didn't belong there. Work had been long and hard, but she wouldn't have it any other way.

Then after work, she spent the evenings with Ridge.

"I will. I'm already missing you." He pressed a quick, hard kiss to her lips and took her hand in his.

Her heart skipped a beat at his words. They walked around to the front of the house, and it was then she realized she didn't see his truck.

"How'd you get here?" she asked. Only her and Aimee's vehicles were in parked out front.

"I left my truck by the barn and walked over. I'll text you later when I'm on my way back." He gave her hand a squeeze before releasing it. He strode away down the path that led to the barn.

She stood in place and watched him for a few

moments, then turned for the bunkhouse. Aimee chose that moment to come out the front door.

"Lover boy left?" she asked.

Melah chuckled and shook her head. "Yeah. He's too damn stubborn. I told him we are fine here."

"Nothing wrong with a man wanting to be overly cautious about the safety of his woman." Aimee tossed her a wink.

Melah rolled her eyes and walked past her so she could run in the house to grab a few things before going to work. "I'll see you later."

Melah jogged in the house and went to her room. She collected a baseball cap and her gun. Everything may have appeared to be back to normal on the ranch, but something in her gut still didn't sit well.

And she always trusted her gut.

"Son of a bitch," Melah muttered. She set the wire cutters down on the ground and glared at the fence she had to mend. Some heifers had broken out of their enclosure and had been found a mile away. She had volunteered to fix the area while the others had rounded up the cattle and moved them. She glanced over her shoulder and found Daisy grazing off in the distance near a wooded area. They were far on the eastern side of the ranch, located near the mountains. The views were one of the perks of working this ranch. It went on for miles in one direction while the other led to the great mountain range.

South Dakota was such a breathtaking state.

Melah let out a sigh. There was no point in getting frustrated. She was going to need a few other things to get this fence back right. She'd run and pick up what she needed and come back. It wouldn't take her long. She pushed off the ground and took her hat off to wipe the sweat off her forehead. It was another scorcher. Apparently, Mother Nature was showing off. They'd been experiencing a heat wave for the past couple of weeks. Melah couldn't wait for the winter—almost.

She'd heard the winters here were no joke. This would be her first one to experience, and she didn't mind the snow. It was the coldness she was worried about. She'd heard there'd been days last year where the wind chill factor had hit negative thirty or lower. Looking up at the bright sun beaming down on her, she may take her chances with the cold. She could always bundle up. With this heat, there was only so much she could take off.

"Come on, Daisy." She brushed her hands on the

back of her jeans. She'd leave her tools here. No point in packing up if she was just going to come right back. She ambled over to her faithful horse who didn't have a care in the world. Melah smiled at Daisy. Maybe later they'd go out for a nice long run. Her hoof seemed to be back to normal. She arrived at Daisy's side and gave her a firm pet on the shoulder. "You ready, girl? I promise we'll be a few minutes and then we will come right back."

Daisy lifted her head and shook it. Her eyes were wide as she stepped away from Melah.

What the devil?

"What's wrong, girl?" Melah tried to reach for her reins, but Daisy took another step away from her.

Melah blew out a frustrated breath. She didn't have time for games today. Daisy released a high-pitched neigh and continued to avoid Melah. This was strange. Daisy had never acted this way before. Even when she was in pain she'd come to Melah.

"Stop playing, Daisy. We still have work to do, and after this last fence to mend, we will be done and I promise I will get you a sweet treat."

Melah was starting to feel the fatigue set in from a long day's work. She had a few peppermints back at the barn she could give Daisy. At this point she was not above begging her horse to not play around.

Melah looked at Daisy.

Something was off. This wasn't playful Daisy. She was picking up something. The hairs on the back of Melah's neck rose. She froze in place. Was her horse warning her of something? Melah swallowed hard and tried to act as if nothing was wrong.

"Okay, girl. If you just want to graze a little more, you could have just said so." Melah gave a shaky laugh. It was then she felt eyes on her on. A calmness washed over her. She was not going to let her fear of the unknown take over her. She had learned that from the military. Being in hot zones meant someone was always watching. Someone was always plotting to take them out, and she and her troops had to stay one step ahead of the enemy.

She felt the comfort of her weapon in her thigh sheath.

"A few more minutes, Daisy. Then we have to go." It helped for her to hear her own voice. If there was truly someone watching her, she didn't want to let on that she'd picked up on them. She casually turned around and rested her hands on her waist. She glanced at the sky as if to enjoy the warm sunrays. She smiled slightly and gazed at the scenery to take it in.

At least she wanted to give off the sense she was

admiring the beauty of nature around her, but in reality, she quickly catalogued everything. Her training was ingrained in her.

Her gut was screaming that she and Daisy were not alone and whoever it was, was not friendly.

"Fuck this." Melah reached down and withdrew her weapon from its holster. Her radio was on Daisy. She'd have been able to radio for someone to come to her, but with the way Daisy was spooked, she didn't want to increase her horse's anxiety and risk getting hurt in the process.

Melah aimed her gun true and stalked toward the woods. She didn't know what she was going to find, but she damn sure was going to clear the area.

For all she knew it could be a predator who was stalking her horse. If so, she'd protect Daisy and put down whatever wolf or mountain lion that waited for her. There had been reports in the last weeks of small game disappearing from the local ranches and being blamed on the wild animals hunting.

She crept into the woods, thankful it was still daytime where she had good lighting. Her hand remained steady. It may have been a while since she'd gone into a hot situation, but her training hadn't faded. Her gaze swept over the tall trees, bushes, and wildflowers of the wooded area.

Was she crazy?

No. Her gut never led her wrong, and she doubted it would start now.

"If you don't want to get shot, you'll show yourself," Melah called out. She flipped off the safety and swung around at a slight snapping sound. She tightened her grip on her weapon. "Now."

She hardened her voice. She was not here to play, she was dead serious. She'd shoot and ask questions later. She took a few more steps forward along a path and swung around again.

A force came at her and hit her arms, her gun lowering. A gasp escaped her. She automatically fell into a defensive move.

Again—training still intact.

Her eyes widened at the person standing in front of her.

"Miss me?" Theo grinned. He was dressed in fatigues which had allowed him to blend in with nature. He even had dark paint on his face. His hair was slicked back away from his face.

"What the fuck are you doing here?" she snapped. She went to raise her gun again with clear intent. It was without a doubt that he was not here just to visit. The crazed look in his eyes alluded to his intentions.

He dove forward just as she pulled the trigger. The sound of the shot echoed through the air.

Shit.

He'd caused her aim to be off and directed at the sky. His body fell against hers, and they landed on the ground. Her gun went flying and disappeared in the brush. Panic washed over Melah, but she fought to push it down. Memories of the last time he'd attacked her came to the forefront.

Not now.

She cried out and fought to shove him off her.

"You thought I would just rot in that damn prison while you get to live the high life?" he growled.

Melah tried to get him off her, but he was solid and too heavy for her.

"Get off me!" she screamed. She swung her arms toward his face. Her nails connected with his cheek and raked down it. Satisfaction filled her at the sight of angry marks appearing on his skin.

"You bitch!" he roared.

The back of his hand connected with her face. Pain seared across her cheek. She cried out but was not going to stop fighting him. Not until there was no breath left in her lungs.

"You are going to pay for that!"

"Help!" she screamed. She didn't know if anyone was close by to hear her or the gunshot.

Theo flipped her over, and within seconds he had her hands zip tied behind her. She continued to struggle and fight against him. She opened her mouth to scream again, but a dirty rag was stuffed into her mouth. She tried to shake it out, but he used something else to wrap around her head to keep it in place. He tore her hat off and tossed it aside.

Tears blurred her vision. She cursed internally at them. This was not the time to cry. Everything he'd put her through before, she had never let him see her cry. Not in court. Not when he was sentenced and he was cursing her out. She'd been strong.

"You are coming with me," he growled in her ear.

He licked it and barked a laugh when she jerked away. He stood and lifted her by her restrained arms. She haphazardly got to her feet. If he thought she was going to just comply because her hands were restrained and she was gagged, he had better think again.

She ran forward but was jerked back to him. She screamed into the cloth.

"Oh, you are not going anywhere." He barked another laugh. He pulled her back to him and wrapped an arm around her chest. His mouth came to hover next to her ear.

She screamed every curse word she could think of at him.

"Still feisty, I see. Well, I'm going to have to break that out of you this time. Let's go, and don't try no funny shit."

He produced a large hunting knife for her to see. He brought the tip of the blade to her cheek, and she froze in place. Another laugh escaped him.

"That's what I'm talking about. Be on your best behavior, and I may give you a little treat." He released her and gripped her by her upper arm and dragged her farther into the woods. "You and I have some unfinished business."

Chapter Sixteen

He's out of prison.

Ridge eyed the text message from his brother. This wasn't the news he'd wanted to hear. He was going to have to let Melah know this. It would appear she hadn't known this information.

Any idea where he is? Ridge shot back. This wasn't good news. Melah was going to freak out when she heard.

No one has seen him in weeks. He's a ghost.

Fuck.

He ran a hand along his face. He didn't want to give her bad news like this, but she had a right to know. Until they found where this Theo was, she was going to stay with him. He didn't care how much of a fight she put up, he was not going to compromise her safety. Even though he'd been sleeping outside the bunkhouse, much could happen with him outside. She may be stubborn, but so was he. If he had to hog-tie her and carry her home, then he would.

A loud crack pierced the air, startling the stillness of the ranch.

Ridge froze in place. It wasn't backfire from a vehicle. Not a slamming gate to one of the corrals. That was a gun. He tilted his head slightly, listening. The echo hung in the air for a heartbeat too long. He waited to see if there would be another, but the next shot didn't come.

He stood by his utility vehicle. He'd gone out on all of his farm runs for the day and had just made his way back to Silver Creek. According to Faith, the office was slow and he wasn't needed back unless there was an emergency.

"Did you hear that?" Ridge called out to Trent who was coming out of the toolshed. He brushed his hands on his jeans and looked off in the distance.

"That was definitely a gunshot," Trent confirmed.

There were miles stretched out before them. Where exactly had it come from?

Ridge's stomach gave way. Where was Melah? She'd started carrying her weapon while working. It had never sat right with him, but he understood the nature of her carrying. She knew how to use it, and if that was her firing, there was a reason for it.

"Where's Melah working?" He hopped in the vehicle and started the engine.

"She's out in the eastern pasture fixing a fence. Damn heifers got loose—"

Ridge didn't stay long enough to hear the rest of what Trent said. If she was out there alone, this would be prime time for someone to try something. He pressed down harder on the gas pedal. He knew exactly which pasture Trent was speaking of. It was the one near the woods and the mountain range.

Perfect place to disappear with someone.

"Hold on, babe. I'm coming." He gripped the steering wheel tight now, wishing he'd had his truck. It would be wasting time to go back to switch vehicles. He secretly hoped he was overreacting. What if a coyote was in the area and she was scaring off the animal? Ridge didn't care. He'd ensure she was safe if that was the case and help her fix the damn fence.

An urgency like he'd never known came over him. He cursed and leaned forward as if that would lend speed to the vehicle. He finally arrived at the empty pasture where Trent said she was working. With his heart racing, he scanned the area for her. Daisy was off grazing, but there were no signs of her owner.

Where the hell was Melah?

He made his way over to Daisy. She was a little way away from the woods, but something drew Ridge's attention to them. He drove up near them and cut the engine. He exited the vehicle and ambled over to Daisy.

"Hey, girl. Remember me?" Ridge spoke in a soft, hushed voice. He didn't want to scare her.

The horse lifted her head and eyed him suspiciously. She neighed softly as he ran a hand along her neck. There didn't look to be any signs of trauma to her.

"Where's your momma? Where's Melah?"

She gave a heavy sigh and shook her head before lowering it again to go back to her meal. The fence where Melah was working wasn't finished. Her tools were still on the ground. He bit back a curse and glanced back to the woods. He gave Daisy another heavy pat, then slowly walked toward the woods. He paused and assessed the area. It appeared as calm as any day. Birds chirping and the sounds of nature filling the air.

He narrowed his eyes and walked along the path that had been naturally created. He eyed the ground. Fresh boot marks. They were small—the size of a woman's feet.

Melah.

"What were you doing, babe?" he murmured slowly. He bent down and examined the ground near him.

She'd spun in a circle as if looking for something —or someone. Had it been her who'd pulled the trigger of her gun?

Or had some mysterious person shot her?

There were no signs of blood anywhere. Ridge breathed a sigh of relief. He stood tall and glanced about. He tiptoed around her tracks then froze in place at the sight of larger prints that appeared out of nowhere. Ridge looked up at the tree where the prints began. Whoever had joined her had been hiding in the tree.

Ridge took a few more steps forward and saw the signs of a tussle on the ground. Anger filled him at the sight. He bent down and eyed the ground. He may have been out of the Navy for years, but some things one doesn't forget. His father had also taught him and Draven the art of tracking when they were younger. Andy would take them hunting, and there was plenty for Ridge to read on the ground.

An attacker had ambushed Melah. Ridge assessed the area, and a hint of black metal stuck out from underneath a bush. He stalked over to it and raised the leaves out of the way. It was a Glock.

Melah's gun, and it had been recently fired.

"Son of bitch," Ridge muttered. Someone had taken his woman. He stood upright and held on to her weapon. Whoever it was didn't even try to cover their tracks. He narrowed his eyes on the ground and began to follow them. They were going toward the mountain.

He and his brother knew this land better than anyone. Whoever had taken Melah was going to regret they'd ever stepped foot on to the Silver Creek Ranch. There was truly no place they could hide from him.

The memory of Melah's face came to mind. Her smile. Her laugh. The sight of her face when she reached her climax.

He wanted to see it again. Experience her arms wrapped around his neck as she stared up at him with an alluring smile on her face. After today, she was going to see how crazy he was for her. He'd fallen in love with her. There was no questioning it.

Ridge was not going to hesitate any longer in making sure she knew his true feelings about her. There was not going to be any discussions of her possibly leaving Ironhaven either.

This was Melah's home.

He was her future.

She was not leaving him. He'd show her how much they belonged together. She had to know it already. The chemistry between them should not be ignored. From the moment they were together, Ridge had felt complete. Words truly couldn't express all there was between them, but he knew one thing for certain.

She was his.

He'd find them. They hadn't had much of a head start, and Ridge could catch up with them easily.

A deadly calm overtook him. When he caught up with the person who'd taken Melah, Ridge would deal with them and get his woman back.

Through any means necessary.

* * *

"There's no use in fighting," Theo snapped.

Melah had refused to allow him to kidnap her

easily. She was going to keep fighting him until she couldn't any longer. She glared at him. He led her farther into the woods. She didn't have a clue where they were. All she could tell was they were heading toward the mountains. There was no way she could allow him to take her there.

"Fuck you." Her words were muffled around the cloth in her mouth.

He brayed a laugh and gripped her by the back of the neck. She had never hated anyone in her life until him. This was one person who she had hoped to never see again, but here he was.

Why couldn't he leave her be? If he was out of jail, why didn't he move on with his life?

"I just know you didn't say 'fuck you,'" he snarled.

He tightened his hold on her neck, causing pain. She bit back a wince. She didn't want him to get any satisfaction from hurting her. He'd always got a kick out of hurting the female soldiers in any way he could. With unfair drills to giving them more work to do than the men, he was known as an ass to women.

"This is all your fault, bitch."

Melah glared at him. Her fault? He was the one who couldn't accept that a woman didn't want him.

She had declined his advances, had been as cour-teous as she could be. Told him she was engaged to be married. He'd kept hounding her. Made crude, inappropriate jokes in front of other personnel, but everyone ignored him. No one wanted his wrath when he got pissed.

They kept walking. The woods were growing thicker, and the dirt path was now no more. She had to watch where she stepped for fear of tripping over fallen branches, tree roots, and such. She hoped someone had heard the gunshot. She just wished she had got it off before he dove toward her. She'd have been in her right to shoot him. He also wouldn't be dragging her to some godforsaken area in the wilderness.

What did he want from her?

What unfinished business did they have?

Theo was sick in the head. She didn't know how he had gotten out of prison, but the fact he was here meant he'd been planning this. A shiver went down her spine with the thought of what he had in store for her.

How the hell had he found her?

So many thoughts and questions raced through her head. She stumbled again, and he gripped her by her arm.

"Watch where you are going, bitch." He grinned at her and narrowed his eyes on her.

She shrugged off his hold.

He laughed. "Believe me when I say you're going to be on your back soon enough."

The contents of her stomach threatened to erupt. He was never going to touch her again. If he thought he was going to do what he'd done to her before, he'd better rethink. She'd made herself a promise that no man would take advantage of her. She'd trained hard to ensure she'd never be vulnerable now.

She just needed her hands free.

Melah held her head high as they marched along. She needed to remain focused. She was going to make it out of here. She was not going to be his victim. She had too much to live for. She had in the past, but those plans had changed.

Now she had a new future.

Ridge's smile came to mind. Her heart stuttered with the thought of the man who'd done everything he could to show her how much he was into her and how much he wanted her. Baggage and all, the man was determined to have her.

Shit.

She should have snagged her cell phone from the saddlebags. She'd been so focused on finishing the fence that she hadn't thought to take her phone and put it in her pocket. Of all the days for her to not have her phone on her, it would be today.

Someone would search for her. Thankfully, a few of the guys knew her last whereabouts and hopefully they'd heard the gunshot. Once they realized she was missing, they'd look for her. A sense of hope bloomed in her chest. Someone would tell Ridge she was missing. After his public display in front of the entire ranch, she doubted they would *not* tell him.

She focused on his image. She'd see him again. Hear his laughter, feel his strong arms around her. There would be plenty of days where she'd rest her head on his chest while he slept and listen to the steady drum of his heartbeat.

She had fallen for her cowboy. There was no doubt in her mind that she loved Ridge. She just wished she'd realized it before now. Melah would tell him. Whatever Theo had planned for her—she would survive.

Again.

She didn't know how long they'd been walking. Her arms ached from being tied behind her. She wouldn't complain or show any weakness. She tried to think of good thoughts. The sight of her father's face when he'd picked her up at the airport from the military for the final time came to mind. His face had lit up the second he'd seen her. There was nothing like a father's love.

He'd like Ridge. Melah was sure of it. With the way Ridge was protective of her, and cared for her, Vernon Battle would be pleased. Somehow, she'd get the two of them together. Matter of fact, she wanted Ridge to meet her entire family from her Uncle Billy and Aunt Sherrie, her cousin Athena to her friends Terri, Issac, and Cora. They were all her family and people she loved more than words could explain.

"This way." Theo pushed her in another direction.

She glanced over at him and still couldn't believe he was out of prison. How? He'd only been sentenced a few years ago. It was bad enough that his sentence was lightened because of recommendations the brass had given him. He should be buried underneath the prison for what he'd done to her.

"I see you got yourself a new boyfriend."

"That's none of your business," she snapped. Her voice was muffled around the cloth in her mouth. She spun on him and advanced. The protective nature inside her flared. He wasn't going to set foot near Ridge. "You don't worry about him either."

"Touchy subject, huh." He laughed. He

narrowed his eyes on her and nudged her away from him. He towered over her and had about a good twenty pounds on her.

She'd never understood how he had made rank. He had been a horrible soldier and an even worse leader.

"I could have killed him the other night. I saw him sleeping outside your house. Things not going well? Is he not giving it to you good?"

Melah screamed and lunged toward Theo. He pushed her down to the ground. She fell backward and landed on her butt. She tried to get back up, but he used his foot to offset her motion, sending her sprawling onto her back. She struggled against the ties that held her hands behind her back. If only she could break free. She'd show him she was not the one to mess with. They were no longer in the military now. She didn't have to worry about saving face or her position.

Now they were both citizens.

Theo bent down and grabbed her by her chin. His hateful gaze was laced with ill intent. A shiver rippled through her. What did he have planned for her?

"Oh, don't worry. Your sorry excuse for a man

will find you. It may be a while before they find your carcass, or whatever is left of it. The coyotes and vultures will be making a meal out of you." His menacing grin spread along his face. His eyes hardened as his gaze roamed over her. "You are going to pay, you little bitch. I rotted in a jail cell because you couldn't keep your mouth shut, and your pussy wasn't all that."

"You fucker!" Her muffled scream went unanswered.

He smirked and rose to his feet and looked around. He'd never had her permission. What transpired between them hadn't been consensual. How dare he make it seem as if it was. The man was truly delusional if he thought she'd wanted him. Had wanted his advances. She'd been happy, and everything had been stripped from her because of him. Her sense of worth, her relationships, her career—all of it gone because he'd taken something that was never his.

Every ounce of anger and rage that lingered inside her rose and threatened to explode from her. He didn't deserve to live for what he'd put her through. Breathing this air, walking this earth—he didn't deserve any of it.

Melah glared at him. The moment she was free he'd wish he'd forgotten her when he was in that jail cell. She didn't care what happened to her, but all she knew was that she was going to get revenge.

It was hers to take.

Chapter Seventeen

R idge wasn't far behind them. He could hear a male's voice up ahead. He kept a slight distance behind them to remain hidden. He didn't want them to know he was trailing them. Whoever this fucker was sucked at moving unnoticed.

He was loud, too talkative, and didn't believe in hiding their tracks.

Either this person was stupid or just cocky enough to think no one would go looking for Melah.

That's where he'd gone wrong. His actions would cost him dearly. Coming onto the Silver Creek Ranch was the worse decision this person could have made, and by taking Melah—he'd just signed his death warrant.

Melah was well liked by all of the former soldiers on the ranch. She was like a sister to most of them. Ridge had heard nothing but good things about her from the others and knew once they found out she was missing, they'd be on the hunt for her.

He felt for his phone and sent a text to his brother.

She's missing. I'm tracking her now.

He slid his phone back in his jeans and continued on. He'd bring her home where she belonged. She was his, and the person who'd taken her was going to pay for putting their hands on her, and if she was harmed in any way, only God could help them.

Ridge remained silent, and from the voice that echoed through the air, it would appear to only be one male.

"Keep going, bitch," the voice growled.

A muffled response was faintly heard. Ridge's hands balled into a tight fist. Was Melah gagged? He practically saw red with the thought, but he had to remain cool. He couldn't lose his focus. He had to save her and ensure she was safe.

The woods were thick at the base of the mountain. There were countless caves one could hide in. He knew from experience. They'd camped in a few when he was younger. His father always believed his boys should feel at one with nature. It gave them a better understanding of life, and Ridge appreciated everything his father had instilled in him as a young man. It may have even attributed to his love of helping animals.

About a half a mile up the mountain there was a large cave that was usually abandoned. In the wintertime, some of the wild animals used it to get out of the storms. From the direction they were headed, Ridge assumed that's where the unknown male was taking Melah.

"I've spent a lot of time thinking of this day. You ruined me, bitch. You know what prison does to a man?"

Theo English.

So the fucker had tracked Melah down. Ridge felt the warmth of Melah's weapon on the small of his back. He'd tucked it in the back of his jeans to keep his hands free. He wouldn't need the gun to deal with Theo. His bare hands were all that were needed.

His time in the Navy may not have been extremely long, but there were some things he'd been taught. Hand-to-hand combat had been one of his favorites. Those skills were ingrained in him. Months turned into years. Ridge utilized all of the skills he had been taught. When he'd gotten out of the Navy, he'd promised himself he'd be something other than what they'd trained him to be.

He'd follow his passion. Went to school on the government's dime and made something of himself. He'd used the system to become the man he wanted to be, not who the Navy had wanted him to be.

One thing about deployments, someone was always trying to kill you.

And Ridge had become very proficient in insuring he was the one who lived.

"What did you say? Let you go? Not a chance," Theo let out a harsh laugh.

Ridge quickened his pace. He remained silent as he approached them. He paused behind a wide tree and glanced around it. Through the brush, he spied Melah, and his breath was snatched from him. She was gagged with her hands bound behind her back. Her hair was a tangled mess, there was dirt on her clothes, but the anger brimming from her eyes told him all he needed to know.

"I lost so much time, now it's your turn. While I was in prison, you got to live your life."

She was strong—a survivor. If looks could kill, Theo would be six feet under.

Ridge's gaze flew to the male gripping her arm. He was a few inches shorter than Ridge's six foot two and was on the lean side. His dirty-blond hair was slicked back. He wore fatigues and boots. There was a wickedly large blade strapped to his waist. Ridge didn't even want to imagine what he was planning to do with that weapon. Ridge narrowed his gaze on the man. This was the man who'd caused his woman so much pain. Put his hands on her. Forced himself on her.

Ridge inhaled, and his entire body trembled.

She'd never have to deal with this Theo again after today. Ridge would ensure it.

Theo guided her out of the wooded area. Ridge stayed back. There was an opening between the woods and where the mountain began. The path up this part of the mountain was rough and rocky. The terrain was not friendly at all. It was harsh, and Melah would have a hard time going up if she didn't have the use of her arms.

"Maybe once I'm done with you, I'll go and visit your good ol' daddy. Make him pay for the sins of his daughter," Theo threatened.

Melah spun on Theo and rammed her shoulder into his stomach. He fell back a few steps in surprise then roared. He shoved her away from him, then advanced on her and drew his hand back. Ridge froze in place for a brief moment. Theo's palm connected with the side of her face and sent her flying down on the ground.

Enough was enough.

Ridge moved.

Theo was his.

Falling to the ground was just what Melah needed. She landed on her ass with a thud. She brought her legs up and slipped her arms over them to bring them in front of her. Her face stung, but it had been worth it. She'd needed to piss him off enough for him to shove her down. The slap hadn't been expected, but at least she was able to get on the ground to get her arms in front of her. She reached down for her pant legs while keeping her gaze locked on Theo.

"You bitch. Fuck my plans. I'll just end you now," he snarled.

He snatched the large blade from its sheath on his waist and strode toward her. She snagged the hem of her jeans and dragged it up. She gripped the small blade she kept strapped to her ankle and brought it out. She rolled onto her knees.

"That little knife is not going to help you."

A crashing sound came from the woods. From the corner of her eye she saw a figure burst from the thicket of trees.

Ridge.

"Back away from her," Ridge snapped.

Her heart fluttered. Theo glanced at Ridge and threw his head back and laughed. She, in the meantime, worked on cutting the ties that bound her hands together. With a few swipes of her blade, the binding fell off her wrist. Relief filled her at being free. Her wrists had been going numb from how tight the binding had been. She snatched the binding and the cloth from her mouth.

"You think you can save this bitch? I should have taken you out when I had the chance the other night," Theo threatened. He got down in a defensive stance and motioned to Ridge with his blade. "I'll deal with your boyfriend, Melah. I'll gut him while you watch."

Ridge's gaze was narrowed on Theo. Melah pushed up from the ground and tightened her grip on her knife.

"You can't take both of us on at the same time." She wasn't going to allow Ridge to fight her battle for her. This was her fight. Theo had come for her, and she'd be damned if Ridge got hurt in the process.

"Stay back, Melah," Ridge warned. His eyes didn't move from Theo. His face was devoid of all emotions.

"Such a gentleman. Doesn't want his woman in a fight. Don't you know, she's a fucking soldier?" Theo snickered.

"I'll never forget it, but she doesn't need to get her hands dirty today." Ridge advanced on Theo with a confident stride.

Melah's gaze flicked between both of the men. Ridge had more height and weight on Theo, but she knew from experience that Theo never fought fair. One of his training highlights had been for them to get dirty and use any means necessary to win in hand-to-hand combat.

"Ridge—" Melah paused at the sight of Ridge's hand slicing down in a hard motion.

He was shutting her down. She stood with her heart in her throat as the two men circled each other. Theo clenched his blade and dove at Ridge. She bit back a scream, but there was no point. Ridge expertly dodged the attack and sent an uppercut to Theo's jaw which landed.

Theo stumbled back and grinned, revealing his

blood-coated teeth. He turned and spat out the dark-crimson fluid. He shook his head.

"Lucky hit. Won't happen again." His smiled disappeared.

He struck toward Ridge again. This time the two men were engaged in a heated fight. Melah swallowed hard around the lump in her throat. She felt so damn helpless watching Ridge battle Theo, but it was soon revealed that Theo had bitten off more than he could chew.

Ridge at first allowed Theo to get a few moves in. A pure assessment of Theo's fighting skills which were lacking compared to his. Ridge then went in like a storm blowing in. His movements were swift and precise. Theo swung his knife at Ridge, but he blocked the move. He brought his fist down on Theo's arm, disarming him. The knife fell to the ground. Ridge somehow kicked it out of the way. Melah dove down to grab it. She didn't want to chance Theo getting his hands on it. She crawled away. The love of her life faced the man she hated. She slid her small dagger back into the sheath on her ankle and gripped Theo's hunting knife. It was large, serrated, and perfect for doing damage to flesh.

They both ignored her and continued to swing at each other. Theo's movements were jerky and unformed, while Ridge was calm and calculated. Ridge pushed Theo away who came back flying at him with a loud roar. Ridge's boot landed in the middle of Theo's stomach and sent him sprawling on the ground.

"Stay down," Ridge snapped.

He stood above Theo who glared at him with such devilish menace it sent a chill down Melah's spine. His face was bloodied with his left eye swelling quickly. It was then Ridge's gaze flicked over to her. It roamed her swiftly, leaving her breathless. She pushed up off the ground with Theo's knife in her hand.

Love for this man filled her.

There were a few scratches on his face, his knuckles were battered and bloodied, but otherwise he remained unharmed.

"Are you hurt?" Ridge asked.

"I'll be fine," she replied.

Her face still throbbed from where Theo had hit her, but it was nothing compared to what could have happened had Ridge not arrived. He strode around Theo and came to her. He cupped her chin, tilted her face to the side, and visually examined her. She was sure a bruise was settling in on her cheek. A darkness filled his eyes as they focused on her cheek.

"Your woman can take a lot." Theo's grim chuckle sliced through the air.

Ridge froze in place. He tilted his head to the side and eyed Theo.

"What the fuck did you just say?" Ridge growled.

"No, Ridge. He's just goading you." Melah rested her hands on his chest to try to keep him away from Theo. The glint in his eyes was different. She'd never seen him like this before.

"I want to hear what the fuck he's got to say." He strode forward, but trying to push him away was like trying to get a stubborn bull to move.

Theo leaned over and spat out more blood.

"I said your woman knows how to take pain. She's a screamer." He rolled over and pushed off the ground.

It was then she took in the sight of a pistol in his hand leveled on her. Melah automatically reached for her gun, but her sheath was empty on her thigh. Ridge shoved her out of the way. She stumbled from the force and fell to the ground.

A resounding crack split the air.

"Ridge!" she screamed. Her gaze fell on Ridge but found him standing with a familiar gun in his hand aimed at Theo.

Theo fell to the ground, holding his thigh. She raced over to Ridge who lowered her gun. Where he'd found it, she didn't know, but she was glad he had. Ridge strode over to Theo and kicked his gun out of his reach.

"This is the last time I'm going to tell you to stay down and shut the fuck up," Ridge barked.

"Why? What are you going to do? You're a lame-ass shot. You should have killed me. I'll never stop coming for the bitch. She deserves to die. I'll make sure it'll be a slow death where she feels all the pain. You'll find her body parts piece by piece."

Ridge raised the gun again and this time aimed at Theo's head.

"No!" she screamed.

She moved swiftly to his side and reached for his arm. She tried to pull it down, but he nudged her away. She scrambled back to him to get the gun. She didn't want him to do something they'd both regret. He was too lost in his rage. She'd seen the look on other soldiers' faces before.

"He's not worth it."

"Do you always do what your woman tells you? You don't have the balls to shoot me again," Theo sneered. The man must have a death wish, but he was not going to get his wish at the expense of her man getting locked up for life.

"Don't listen to him, Ridge," she pleaded.

"Ridge!" a voice shouted from behind them. Draven emerged from the woods. The elder Harvey brother went toward them. "Put the gun down."

"He threatened to kill her," Ridge responded in a monotone. He had yet to take his eyes off Theo.

Worry filled her that Ridge was too far gone. She moved to him, but Draven shook his head. He arrived at Ridge's side and forced his brother's arm down. He took the gun from Ridge's hand.

"Leave. Take her to get checked out. The authorities and an ambulance are on their way," Draven calmly announced. He guided Ridge toward her.

Ridge hesitated at first, but something appeared in Draven's eyes. There was a silent exchange between brothers.

Draven jerked his head toward Melah. "She needs medical attention. See to your woman."

"Who the fuck are you?" Theo snapped. He leaned over and spat again. "If anyone needs medical attention, it's me. He shot me. I want to press charges."

Ridge came to her and gathered her into his arms.

She leaned into his embrace and breathed him in. The strength of him surrounded her, and she never wanted to leave. A heavy sigh released from her. She was so thankful for him. He knew she didn't need him to fight her battle for her, but he'd done so anyway.

"Get up," Draven ordered.

The tone was chilling, and she glanced over at them. Draven reached down and practically lifted Theo from the ground.

"Let's go," Ridge's voice rumbled from his chest.

She nodded and slipped her hand into his waiting one. He tugged her behind him as they walked toward the woods. She glanced over her shoulder at Draven leading a hobbling Theo in another direction.

"Who the fuck are you?" Theo hollered.

"Your worst fucking nightmare," Draven replied.

Melah's head snapped back to Ridge. She didn't know what that meant, but Theo had a new problem on his hands.

Draven.

Ridge guided her along in the woods until they came out onto a path. He stopped abruptly and spun toward her. He brought her to him and lowered his head. His lips overtook hers in a hard kiss. He held her face in his hands, his mouth gently moving over hers. She leaned up on her toes and met his kiss.

"I love you, Melah," Ridge murmured. His lips brushed hers. He rested his forehead on hers.

She wrapped her arms around his neck. His words only confirmed his actions. She'd known he'd had feelings for her, but hearing his admission of love was the icing on the cake.

"I love you, too, Ridge. Thank you for coming to my rescue," she said.

A small smile appeared on his face. He leaned down and pressed another soft kiss to her lips. This man had been willing to kill for her, but that wasn't what she wanted. She needed him in her life—forever.

And not behind prison bars.

"You didn't need me to rescue you, I'm sure, but I'll always have your back." He lifted his head and gently took her chin in his grasp. He tilted it to the side and turned her face away so he could assess her again. "I'm just sorry I didn't get to you quick enough."

"Don't apologize for anything. It's not your fault. Plus I figured he was going to hit me. It was sort of the plan," she admitted sheepishly. Her plan had worked. It had allowed her to free herself.

"Come. Let's get you checked out." He took her hand again and began walking.

She glanced around and didn't recognize any markers she'd seen before when Theo was dragging her through the woods. She wasn't going to question the direction they were going. She was sure Ridge knew the way.

"But what about Draven and Theo? Won't the cops need to know where they're going to be?" She glanced back over her shoulder and didn't see any signs of the two. Nor did she hear anything aside from a few birds calling out.

"What cops?" Ridge asked.

Melah blinked. Was she tripping? Didn't Draven say the authorities were on their way? She remembered the look on Draven's face and decided she didn't even want to know.

Theo was no longer her problem.

Chapter Eighteen

"I'm fine. I don't need medical attention." Ridge waved off the EMT, Raymond, who offered to look at his hands.

As Draven had promised, they had been waiting for them. All Ridge had been concerned about was Melah and making sure she was unharmed. He hadn't been surprised when she'd admitted she had planned to take a hit. When he'd first seen her with Theo her hands had been behind her, so it was apparent she'd needed to get down on the ground to bring them in front of her.

His woman was smart and strong. Not many would risk getting hit on purpose. He glanced at her in the back of the ambulance. Apparently, they'd been called out for an accident on the ranch. A few of the hands were standing around. They'd been alerted to Melah's disappearance. By the time he and Melah had exited the woods, Trent, Ethan, Aimee, and a few others were on their way in and they'd all been armed and ready for battle.

"Thanks. I promise I don't need to go to the hospital." Melah smiled at the other medic who was checking her blood pressure. "I've fallen off a horse plenty of times."

The medic's eyebrows rose sharply at her excuse.

"Um, okay." He finished her vitals and announced she was fine. "Well, if you feel dizziness, double vision, or have an extreme headache that doesn't go away, call us immediately and we'll transport you to the hospital."

"Of course. Thank you so much. You have been wonderful." She stood off the stretcher and walked toward the edge of the truck.

Ridge met her and held out his hand to her. She took it and hopped down on the ground. He brought her close to him and gave a nod to the two medics.

"Take care of her, Doc," Raymond said.

"Always." He rested his hand on the small of Melah's back. He couldn't keep his hands off her. It was going to be a long time before he'd feel comfortable letting her out of his sight.

"Everyone good?" Andy asked.

He and Buck exited his truck. His gaze swept over the both of them. Ridge hadn't realized they'd pulled up.

"We're fine," he said.

"I'm okay." Melah leaned into his hold.

He couldn't wait to get her back to his house. They both were covered in dirt and needed to shower. She was not going anywhere but to his house. Damn the bunkhouse. Not tonight and not ever again. After today, she was moving in with him. He wasn't going to take any other answer but yes this time.

"Where's Draven?" Andy took a look at the few standing around.

The ambulance driver blew their horn and took off down the road. Buck moved over to the hands and spoke with them. Andy came to stand in front of Melah and Ridge.

"Taking out the trash," Ridge replied automatically. He hadn't questioned his brother at all.

Draven would take care of Theo, and Ridge couldn't care less in which way. As long as Melah was safe, that was all that mattered. His father gave a satisfied nod.

"Good. Y'all get cleaned up. Bee has some

dinner waiting for you. We'll bring it up to your house." Andy tilted his nod to Melah. "If you need anything, Melah, don't hesitate to ask."

"Yes, sir." She wrapped her arm around his waist.

Ridge tightened his hold on her. He dropped a kiss on the top of her head. His family had accepted her with him.

"Come on. Let's go home." He led her over to his truck and helped her in. Once he'd secured her with her safety belt, he jogged over to his side. It didn't take long to drive from the main barn over to his home.

Once they crossed over the threshold of his front door, he slammed it shut and pushed her up against the door. He stood before her with only a few centimeters separating them.

"This is your home." He wanted to ensure she knew where her place was going to be. He was ready for an argument, but it didn't come.

"It is. Wherever you are is where I belong," she announced.

Her big brown eyes were wide and filled with love. He leaned down and covered her lips with his. He could have lost her today. Theo had somehow come onto the ranch unnoticed and apparently had been plotting to do her bodily harm.

I should have taken you out when I had the chance the other night.

Theo's words echoed in his head. The fucker had been casing out the bunkhouse. Ridge pushed down the surge of anger that threatened to erupt. There was no point. Theo English would not bother Melah again.

His woman was safe.

Melah tore her lips from his. They were both breathing heavy. Her gaze dropped down to his hands. Her eyes widened in shock. He looked at his hands and bit back a grimace. The skin on his knuckles was mangled and covered in dried blood. They were already sore and stiff. It was going to be a few days until he'd be able to utilize his hands.

"You need to do something about them." She gently took his right hand in hers and shook her head. "Come. Let's go into the kitchen to get some ice."

"I'll be fine. I'll do that later." He bent down and lifted her into his arms.

She threw hers around his neck and held on. He kicked off his shoes and stalked through the house to the staircase. He took the stairs two at a time while carrying her.

"At least clean them and put something on them so they won't get infected," she exclaimed.

"I will." He nudged the door to his bedroom open and strode through it. He didn't stop until they were in his master en suite. Then he lowered her to her feet. He cupped her face in his hands and dropped a kiss on her lips. "We both need to take a hot shower. I don't know about you, but I feel like I have dirt in my pores."

She glanced over at the mirror and let out a little yelp.

"Okay. Shower first, then you must promise me to let me put something on your knuckles," she said, turning back to him.

"I promise." He went over to the shower and switched the water on to allow it to warm up a bit. When designing the bathroom, he'd ensured it had plenty of space. The shower was a walk-in with a glass wall separating it from the bathtub.

"I don't have any clothes here." She went over the sink and pulled her hair out of the ponytail. She combed her fingers through her tangled strands. She grimaced and continued her attempt to tame her hair.

"I'm sure I have something you can wear." He checked the water and found it to be satisfactory. He tugged at his shirt and raised it over his head. His hand dropped to his belt. He swore at the pain of trying to undo it.

She glanced over and saw he was having a slight issue.

She moved over to him and pushed his hands out of the way.

"Your shirts are way too big." She chuckled. She opened the belt then went to the button of his jeans. She undid it and lifted her gaze to his.

"Well, you need something to cover you when my father and Bee bring the food," he said.

She gave a quick nod then threw her hair up into a bun on the top of her head.

"I guess it will do. But then what?" She drew down his jeans. They fell to the floor.

He kicked them away and stood proudly before her in just his boxer briefs. His cock was thickening. It lifted and pressed against the cotton material. She arched an eyebrow at him and shook her head.

"None of that until I make sure your hands are okay." Melah backed away from him while a sexy grin spread across her face.

"What? Of course not. I can't control him," he muttered.

She removed her clothes, and with each article that fell to the floor, he grew even harder. He released a curse and shucked off his underwear.

"Whatever, Ridge. I know you." She brushed past him and went over to the shower.

Her naked form had him salivating. His cock stood fully erect at the sight of her. She reached in and tested the water herself before walking into the spray of water.

He followed behind her.

The initial spray stung. Especially on his knuckles, but he ignored the pain and gathered Melah in his arms. He positioned them to where his back was to the water. She reached up and entwined her fingers at the base of his neck. They stood there for what seemed like eternity just staring at each other. No words were needed. The water beat down on his back in a rhythmic beat. It felt good, but having Melah in his arms was better.

He was in awe that this woman was his. He'd waited forever to find the right person to spend his life with, and he knew without a doubt Melah was his.

"I love you." He'd never tire of saying the words.

"And I love you." She lowered her forehead to his chest and inhaled sharply.

He ignored his hard cock and brought her closer to him.

"All I could think about when Theo had me was getting back to you," she said.

Ridge's heart thundered. He didn't want to think of the fear that had filled her at the hands of that crazed lunatic. He'd been close to pulling the trigger when Theo was spouting off what he'd done to Melah. The sound of her begging him and then Draven appearing had brought him back to himself.

He'd gone to a place he hadn't ever wanted to go to again.

That was why he'd gotten out of the military. He hadn't wanted to lose himself.

But at that moment looking down at Theo and imagining his hands on Melah, causing her physical pain, imagining her screams...at that moment he'd wanted to end him.

He blinked and came back to the present. He dropped a kiss on the top of her head.

"And all I could think of was getting to you. Melah, you are everything to me." He tilted her chin up to force her to look at him.

The spray landed on her face. She smiled up at him.

"How did I get so lucky? I didn't come here to find love," she admitted. Her small hand slid along his shoulder and came to rest on his chest just above his heart. "I was too busy wanting to figure out my future, but apparently something knew my future was waiting here on this ranch."

"You're damn right I was waiting on you," he playfully growled.

He lowered his head and covered her lips with his. Her worries of finding where she belonged were no more. Her place was here in his arms and his home—*their home*. What was his, was now hers. He looked forward to having her officially move in and putting her touch on the house he'd built.

When he had designed this place, he'd pictured a wife and kids in it with him.

A moan escaped Melah as he tilted his head to deepen the kiss. Her soft mounds were crushed between them. He slid his hand down her back and cupped her ass. There was no room between them. His cock was pressed against her stomach. He tore his mouth from hers and trailed it along her cheek. He continued on to nuzzle her neck. He walked them backward until her back was leaning on the wall.

"Ridge. Your father will be here soon," she gasped.

He nipped the sensitive skin along her neck, eliciting a tremor through her body. He bent down and lifted her. Her legs automatically wrapped around his waist.

"And?" He trailed his tongue along her skin.

Her fingers dove into his hair, sending a shiver down his spine. He moved her higher to position his cock at her entrance.

"Meaning that we don't have time for this. We need to—"

Her words ended in a moan as he brought her down on him. Her pussy opened and accepted him, and he sank completely in her. Ridge groaned at her tightness. He paused and gripped her thighs to hold her in place.

"What was that?" he asked.

He inhaled sharply at how tight she was wrapped around him. Her silky warmth was slick and coated his cock. Melah always took him perfectly. Being buried inside her was where he belonged. His cock swelled even more.

"I said we need to hurry," she gasped.

She leaned her head back on the wall. Her eyes were closed. She was the most beautiful woman he'd ever seen. He withdrew slightly then thrust again.

He smiled at her change of heart.

Epilogue

"This is Reggie!" Melah exclaimed.

She grinned wide. The large bull calf ambled over to them. Reggie took his time leaving his adoptive mother's side. He hadn't weaned from her yet, and according to Ridge, Reggie would do so when he was good and ready to. His adoptive mother had been so gentle with him. It hadn't mattered that he had a slight deformity. She'd lost her calf, and when they had introduced the two, it was love at first sight.

"Reggie? Why does he have a name and the others don't?" her father, Vernon, asked.

The older man laughed at his daughter, but she didn't care.

"I'm not sure you want to know." Ridge chuckled. He leaned against the fence and folded his arms.

"Let's just say that Reggie and I bonded when he was born." She climbed up on the fence and leaned over to give Reggie a firm rub on his head.

The bull calf bellowed his greeting to them. His eyes were closed, and she scratched behind an ear. The past six months had flown by, and Melah couldn't be any happier.

"Go back with the others, silly boy. I can't stay here and scratch you all day."

She gave him another pat on his head. He opened his eyes and huffed his complaint. The kid had attitude. She laughed and jumped down from the fence.

"I'm glad you are happy here," her father said. He adjusted his veteran ball cap that he always wore proudly. He'd come to the ranch to visit. This was the second time he'd been out to see her.

She went over to him and wrapped her arms around his waist. He squeezed her tight.

"I am. I love it here," she admitted.

She pulled back and eyed Ridge who was smiling at her and her father.

These past six months with Ridge had her realizing she'd never been loved properly before by any man. Pierce was a distant memory now that Ridge had showed her how a man should love a woman. She now appreciated Pierce revealing his true colors. He'd gotten out of the way for her true love to come into her life.

No one spoke of what had happened to Theo. She knew better than to ask. The next time she'd seen Draven he'd been the same strong, silent man who she'd come to know. They worked alongside each other, and not once did he bring up that day.

If he wasn't going to share what had happened after she and Ridge had left, then she wasn't going to ask. Some things were better left unknown.

"I'm glad, but you need to come home soon. Your aunt and uncle are driving me crazy. They think you've forgotten all about them," her father grumbled.

"What? That is not true. I talk to Aunt Sherrie at least every other day, and Uncle Billy is always in the background saying something." She laughed.

Her uncle and aunt were being overly dramatic. When they'd all found out she was staying permanently on the ranch, they'd been concerned, but then they'd met Ridge. She'd gone home a few months ago and had taken him with her.

Her family had fallen for him just as fast as she

had. Anyone could see how much this man loved her. Even Athena joked that maybe she should come spend some time on the ranch so she could find a man.

Melah ambled over to Ridge and leaned against him. When he was near her, she always had the urge to touch him in some way. She inhaled his familiar scent that always calmed her.

"You know how they are. You're like their other daughter." Her father leaned against the fence and stared off into the distance.

"I know. They're more than welcome to come and visit. We have plenty of room here." Melah glanced over at Ridge.

He tossed an arm around her shoulders.

"Would that be all right?" she checked.

"Of course. They're welcome to come any time." He flicked his gaze over at her father.

Something passed between the two of them. She frowned. What the hell was that?

"Melah." Ridge turned to her and gently moved her to stand in front of him. He took her hands in his and brought them up to his lips and pressed a kiss to the back of both of them.

"What are you doing?" She giggled.

She stared over at her father who was just watching them with an amused look. Her smile disappeared at the sight of Ridge getting down on one knee.

She gasped. "Seriously, Ridge. What are you doing?"

"What I've been dying to do for a while." Ridge smirked.

He reached into his jeans pocket and pulled out a little black box. Her heart pounded at the sight of it. He kept a hold of her one hand and flipped open the box to reveal a stunning ring nestled inside. He cleared his throat and tightened his hold on her.

"Melah Battle. Will you do me the honor of becoming my wife?"

"Did you know about this?" She looked at her father who barked a laugh and nodded.

"I did. Now answer the man. Don't leave him hanging," Vernon said.

She turned back to Ridge who was patiently waiting for her answer. Love filled her at the sight of her man on his knee. He was her entire world. She hadn't been truly living until she'd met him. She couldn't imagine her life without him and didn't want to.

There was only one answer for the man who loved her with every breath in his body.

"Yes."

Thanks for reading book nine of the Silver Creek Ranch series! Up next is Her Missing Cowboy by L. Loren! Make sure you snag the next book today!

A Note From the Author

Dear reader,

Thank you for reading Falling For Her Cowboy! I had a lot of people asking if Ridge was going to get his book after they read Draven's book, Wrangling Her Cowboy. Of course the youngest Harvey brother was going to get his happy ever after!

I hope you enjoyed Ridge and Melah. It was such a pleasure to watch their story unfold. Silver Creek Ranch has touched the lives of so many cowboys, I hope you stick around and read the rest of this season! My author friends were so excited to be able to be apart of this project! We have a total of TEN books joining this world this year.

Please don't forget to leave a review and/or rating for this book once you are done reading!

Happy reading,
Peyton Banks

P.S. If you didn't read the first season, books 1-8, please go back and grab those today and read them in between the new season!

Her Missing Cowboy
Silver Creek Ranch 10

When his trail goes cold, her broken heart guides her.

Being the only female Marine Raiders can be isolating. Finding love was almost impossible. When a sexy civilian contractor catches her eye, Cassidy Jacks finds her loneliness dissipating. However, when that connection is unexpectedly severed, she is left heartbroken and alone... again.

Forced to take an overseas job to save his family's orchard, Joaquin Tanner finds himself surrounded by danger. What he didn't expect was to meet his soul mate. When a random act of violence rips his whole world apart, the cowboy finds himself in the fight of his life. The result leaves him maimed and doubting his self-worth.

Though Silver Creek Ranch is a haven for veterans, his military buddy convinces Mr. Harvey to make an exception for a fellow rancher. The ranch works its magic to not only bring Joaquin back to life, but also to heal his heart in the process.

When the love of her life goes missing, Cassidy is determined to find him, no matter what sacrifices she must make, including giving up her thriving military career. However, when the search is over, she finds the work has just begun.

Her Missing Cowboy is the next book in the Silver Creek Ranch series.
Grab your copy of Her Missing Cowboy today!

About the Author

USA TODAY bestselling author, Peyton Banks, is the alter ego of a city girl who is a romantic at heart. Her mornings consist of coffee and daydreaming up the next steamy romance book ideas. She loves spinning romantic tales of hot alpha males and the women they love. Make sure you check her out!

Sign up for Peyton's Newsletter to find out the latest releases, giveaways and news! Visit www.peytonbanks.com/newsletter to sign up!

Want to know the latest about Peyton Banks? Follow her online:

tiktok.com/@peytonbanks_author

facebook.com/peytonbanksauthor

goodreads.com/peytonbanks

bookbub.com/profile/peyton-banks

instagram.com/peytonbanks_author

Also by Peyton Banks

Country at Heart

Cowboy, Take Me Away

Hard to Forget

Lasso My Heart

<u>Special Weapons & Tactics Series</u>

Dirty Tactics (Special Weapons & Tactics 1)

Dirty Ballistics (Special Weapons & Tactics 2)

Dirty Operations (Special Weapons & Tactics 3)

Dirty Alliance (Special Weapons & Tactics 4)

Dirty Justice (Special Weapons & Tactics 5)

Dirty Trust (Special Weapons & Tactics 6)

Dirty Secrets (Special Weapons & Tactics 7)

Dirty Ultimatum (Special Weapons & Tactics 8)

<u>SWAT boxset, books 1-3</u>

<u>SWAT boxset, books 4-6</u>

<u>Trust & Honor Series (BWWM)</u>

Dallas

Dalton

<u>A Langdale Christmas</u>

The Christmas Secret

The Christmas Wish

The Christmas Gift

The Christmas Wonder

<u>Interracial Romances (BWWM)</u>

Pieces of Me

Hard Love

Retain Me

Silent Deception

Surgeon Book Boyfriend

<u>African American Romance</u>

Breaking The Rules

<u>Mafia Romance</u>

Unexpected Allies (The Tokhan Bratva #1)